Deer in the Darkness

Ben M. Baglio

Illustrations by Ann Baum

**Cover illustration by
John Butler**

AN
APPLE
PAPERBACK

SCHOLASTIC INC.

New York Toronto London Auckland Sydney
Mexico City New Delhi Hong Kong Buenos Aires

Special thanks to Tanis Jordan

No part of this publication may be reproduced in whole or in part, or stored in a retrieval system, or transmitted in any form or by any means, electronic, mechanical, photocopying, recording, or otherwise, without written permission of the publisher. For information regarding permission, write to Working Partners Limited, 1 Albion Place, London W6 0QT, United Kingdom.

ISBN 0-439-52103-3

12 11 10 9 8 7 6 5 4 3 2   4 5 6 7 8/0

Printed in the U.S.A.   40

First Scholastic printing, March 2003

One

"Feel the weight of that!" Dr. Adam Hope said, passing the gleaming metal helmet to James.

James took it eagerly and whistled. "Armor weighs a ton!" He gasped.

Mandy laughed. She and James hadn't been very interested when Dr. Adam had suggested they visit Cranbourne Park, a historic stately home that opened its doors to the public in the summer. But now they were really enjoying the guided tour.

"I can't imagine even *wearing* something as heavy as this," Mandy said as James handed the helmet to her, "let alone fighting a battle in it."

"That was the trouble with suits of armor," the tour guide told them. "Once a knight was fully dressed, he was so heavy he could hardly walk."

"How did they get on their horses?" James asked, frowning.

"I know the answer to that," Dr. Emily Hope answered. "They lifted them up with a hoist. Isn't that true, Tilly?" she said to the guide.

"That's it exactly," Tilly replied.

"But what if they fell off?" Mandy asked. She grinned at the thought of a knight in armor lying on his back, waving his legs in the air like a stranded beetle.

"They'd usually have a servant nearby," Tilly explained. "But if they didn't" — she shrugged her shoulders and looked serious for a moment — "then that's when they would be most vulnerable to the enemy."

Mandy studied the helmet for a moment. "I think this would be a bit too small for you, Dad!" she teased.

"My head's not *that* big!" Dr. Adam laughed.

"It probably is compared to people hundreds of years ago," Tilly told him. "On the whole, people were much smaller then." She took the helmet from Mandy and fitted it back onto the shoulders of the suit of armor. "Shall we go to the portrait gallery now?" She set off along the long, oak-paneled corridor.

"Look, Mandy!" James called as they started to follow Tilly. "I bet this would almost fit me."

Mandy turned to see James standing beside the suit of armor, measuring his height against it. "You're right, James," she said, nodding in agreement. "I see what Tilly meant about people being smaller. Wouldn't it be fun to try it on?"

"I don't think so," James replied. "If it's anything like the helmet, I wouldn't be able to stand up!"

Mandy walked over to the window, knelt on the padded window seat, and looked out. "It's still raining," she observed. The view down the long, tree-lined drive was gray and dreary. Drizzle hung in the trees, making them look as if they were full of fog.

Mandy's parents were taking a week's vacation from Animal Ark, their busy veterinary clinic in Yorkshire. Mandy's best friend, James Hunter, had been invited along, too. Simon, the clinic nurse, had agreed to hold the fort with a substitute vet and had even recommended a stone cottage in Northumberland where he sometimes stayed himself. Since their arrival, the Hopes had been out and about every day, watching gray seals from a boat and visiting the local horse shows as well as exploring the lofty, windswept moorland.

"The rain doesn't really matter," James said as he

joined Mandy by the window. "It's good here, and Tilly makes it interesting. Anyway, look!" He pointed to a break in the gray clouds. "There's a patch of blue sky over there."

"Let's hope the rain clears up soon," said Mandy. "Come on, we'd better catch up." She jumped off the window seat and walked along the corridor to a door at the far end.

The portrait gallery was empty when Mandy and James entered. Their tour group had already moved on to the room beyond.

Mandy stopped before the first picture. "James, come and look at this!" she said, motioning him over. The picture in front of her was a life-size painting of a man in an ornate gold frame. His eyes were very dark, and his lips were set in a thin line.

"*The first Lord Dunstan of Cranbourne*," James read from the caption on the bottom of the frame. "It's very old. The date says 1603, or it could be 1608."

"Imagine wearing clothes like that!" Mandy said, wrinkling her nose.

The man wore blue velvet knickers and a white shirt with flowing sleeves. A sash of gold braid was draped across his chest, and around his neck was a stiff white lace ruff.

"It looks almost as uncomfortable as the armor," James remarked, opening their guidebook and flicking through the pages to the portrait section. "It says here that the first Lord Dunstan was a Knight of the Garter. Apparently, King James stopped at Cranbourne Park on his way down from Scotland to take the English throne and gave him the title to thank him for his hospitality."

Mandy moved down the room. "Hey, James, look at *this* one," she said, stopping in front of a smaller painting. A man was holding the reins of a horse with two tiny dogs standing next to it. The dogs had smooth, light brown bodies, short legs, and tiny mouselike faces.

"What kind of dogs are they?" James wondered.

"I don't know," Mandy confessed. "They don't look like any breed I've seen before." She took the guidebook from James to see if it had any more information.

"I think they're terriers," said a voice behind them.

Mandy and James spun around. A blond young man was standing in the doorway, smiling at them. "It's the style of painting that makes them look a little strange," he explained. "Though it *was* very fashionable to have small dogs in those days — but not as small as that, I think."

Mandy noticed that he had an accent. "I think he's an American tourist," she whispered to James.

"I wouldn't like riding a horse in those clothes, would you?" the young man continued, walking into the room and studying the picture.

Mandy and James looked at the painting. The man holding the horse wore a tight-fitting armor top and armor-fronted trousers that stopped at the knee. From his expression, Mandy thought he looked uncomfortable.

"He does look a little miserable!" James said with a grin. Then he leaned forward and peered closely at the painting. "These men are all wearing the same ring," he commented. He pointed to a chunky gold ring that the figure was wearing on the little finger of his left hand. "It looks like it's got some sort of crest on it."

The ring was topped with an ornate red crest, but it was too small in the painting to tell what it was.

"It must have to do with the knighthood. These were all Lord Dunstans at some time," Mandy explained to the young man, who didn't seem to have a guidebook.

"Really?" He grinned at her. "But I don't look like any of them!"

Mandy looked puzzled. "I don't see why you'd want to," she said. "They all seem so grumpy, and the first Lord Dunstan even looks a little mean." She looked up at the first painting again and narrowed her eyes.

"Mandy, come and look," James called to her from the corner by the door. "This Lord Dunstan looks nice, and he has a good-looking dog."

With a sideways glance at the young man, Mandy walked over to James, flicking through the guidebook until she found the picture James was looking at. A smiling, middle-aged man wearing a dark suit stood under a beech tree. One hand rested on the head of an elegant black-spotted dog.

"It says here this is the current Lord Dunstan," Mandy said, lowering her voice as if she expected him to walk in.

"Yes, but he's not the current Lord Dunstan," the young man said, walking over and joining them.

Mandy frowned and looked up. She pointed to the picture in the guidebook. "He is," she told him. "Look, it says so here."

The young man sighed and ran a hand through his blond hair. "The guidebook hasn't been updated yet," he explained. "I know it must be confusing, but I've got a list of jobs as long as your arm."

"Do you work here?" James asked him, throwing a curious glance at Mandy.

"Sort of." The man looked embarrassed. "And you are —?" He put out his hand.

"Mandy Hope," Mandy said, taking his hand and shaking it. "And this is James Hunter. We're on a tour of the house — only we seem to have been left behind."

"Well, I suppose I *do* work here," he said, looking up at the painting again. His eyes filled with sadness. "That picture *was* the last Lord Dunstan. He was my father. He died last year."

"I'm sorry," Mandy said at once, and then she stopped. Her eyes widened and she stared at him. "Then you must be —"

"Lord Dunstan of Cranbourne, at your service," the young man said with a bow. His face broke into a warm smile. "But you can call me Will."

Two

Mandy stared at the man, feeling a rush of embarrassment wash over her. He was Lord Dunstan, and they'd been saying such dreadful things about his ancestors! She glanced at James, her cheeks flaming. Quickly, she tried to collect herself. "I'm very sorry," she sputtered. "We didn't really mean to be rude. They *are* your ancestors, after all."

"That's right," James said. "I'm sure they were all very — er — very —" He searched for a word and looked desperately at Mandy, who thought for a few seconds.

"Worthy!" Mandy exclaimed, feeling very pleased with herself.

Will laughed. "I'm sorry. I should have told you earlier, but I couldn't resist teasing you," he said as he gestured toward the paintings with his hand. "You've cheered me up a lot. The thing is, you're both right. Most of them do look pompous and grumpy."

"Except your dad," Mandy offered, relief flooding through her. At least there hadn't been anything uncomplimentary to say about the man with the Dalmatian.

"Except my dad," Will agreed, nodding his head. "He was a good man, but he wasn't always the best judge of character. I think people sometimes took advantage of his good nature." Mandy and James were silent as Will stared around the room. "Still, there's not much that we can do about the others now, is there?" he said briskly, recovering himself. "I must make sure my portrait looks cheerful when it's done."

"You have the same ring as the other lords," James remarked, noticing that the big gold ring on Will's little finger had a familiar-looking red crest. "I didn't see it before."

"I kept that hand in my pocket, James," Will admitted, "so I wouldn't give myself away. Each lord gives a replica of the ring to his eldest son on his twenty-first birthday. I've never taken it off."

"Does the ring have a meaning?" Mandy asked, curious.

"It used to, years ago," said Will, holding his hand out so they could examine it. "When a lord signed a document he would melt some sealing wax beside his signature and press the ring into it. When the wax dried, it would show the crest. Look, it's a stag's head with a sword." He looked thoughtful for a moment, then continued. "Of course, sealing wax doesn't carry much weight in this day and age, but my father still used his ring on official documents." Will gazed at his father's portrait for a moment and took a deep breath. Talking about the ring seemed to remind him of something sad.

Mandy thought his face looked very troubled. "Shall we move on?" she suggested softly to James. "We don't want to bother Will."

"No, don't worry, I'm OK," Will said quickly. "I'm just glad Tilly called me in time so that I could get back to England while my father was still alive."

"Where were you?" James asked, puzzled.

"I was working in the United States," Will replied. "But then Dad got sick and he asked Tilly to track me down. At least I managed to see him before he died."

"So will you go back to the States now?" asked Mandy.

Will shook his head solemnly. "No. I'm back, and the estate needs me. I'm Lord Dunstan now, and there's a lot to take care of."

Before Mandy or James could ask him anything more,

he put a hand on each of their shoulders and steered them back into the corridor. "Come on, you can meet up with the tour group later. First, I'll show you the best thing in the house," he said. He led them along the corridor and opened one of the doors with a flourish. It led into a narrow passageway, lit with lamps shaped like candles set into the walls. "Follow me!"

Mandy and James exchanged glances as they hurried after him. Will was striding confidently along, his shoes squeaking on the wooden floorboards. The passage led into a broad, carpeted hallway. They passed comfortable-looking armchairs and tables dotted with framed photographs.

"This is the private wing of the house," Will told them. "This is where the family lives, or at least where *I* live. It's a shortcut to the room we want." He turned a corner and took them through a doorway and up a flight of stairs, stopping in front of an elaborately carved door. Opening the door, Will ushered them inside.

Mandy felt a quiver of excitement as she wondered what they were about to see.

"You need to look straight ahead," Will suggested as he let the door swing closed and the room became pitch-black.

Mandy could hear him fiddling with switches behind them. Suddenly, several spotlights flickered on, dim at first but gradually growing brighter. Mandy could hear soft, lilting music in the background. And then, as the room became filled with light, she saw that they were standing in front of a magnificent tapestry that covered one whole wall. The scene depicted a clearing in a forest, full of animals, trees, and people in clothing from many centuries ago.

Mandy and James gasped in amazement.

"Who are the people, and what are they doing?" Mandy asked after a few moments.

"It's King James and his hunting party," Will began. "When the king stayed here the first time, he enjoyed it so much that the lord at the time decided to turn it into one of the king's regular hunting forests. He brought in the fastest, most handsome red deer he could find, and soon our herd was the best in the country. This tapestry shows one of the first royal hunts."

"I suppose hunting was really popular back then," Mandy said.

"That's right, Mandy," said Will. "And the kings were always provided with the best places to hunt." Walking up to the tapestry, he pointed to a figure with a ginger-colored mustache and beard who was mounted on a big black horse. Standing on either side of him were men with bows and arrows in their hands, and behind them were other men on horses. "This is King James," Will said. He gave a little snort. "History says that he was actually fat and ugly, but I don't think anyone dared to depict him like that!"

"He'd probably have them sent to the Tower of London!" James agreed. "That's what they did in those days, wasn't it?"

"Absolutely right," Will said, nodding vigorously. "It was King James who sent Guy Fawkes to the Tower and had him hanged, drawn, and quartered."

"Yuck," Mandy said, giving a shudder. "That's disgusting!"

"Do you know who this is?" Will pointed to a side view of a figure. He was standing under a huge oak tree with spreading branches weighed down by hundreds of tiny green leaves. The man was facing King James, and a tiny fawn was standing behind him.

"That's the first Lord Dunstan!" Mandy exclaimed. "I recognize him from the painting."

"Exactly!" said Will. "You might change your mind about him now, Mandy. Apparently, King James had had very poor hunting that day, and he was in a bad mood. They were just going back when they came across this fawn."

Mandy looked at the fawn, which was standing on a patch of bare earth. The work was so detailed, Mandy could make out each light brown hair on its slender body. Even the earth was faintly marked with delicate hoofprints where the fawn was standing. "But it's gorgeous. Surely King James didn't want to kill the poor little thing?" Mandy felt her scalp prickle, and even though it had happened hundreds of years ago, she really hoped that Will wasn't about to tell her the worst.

"He did," Will admitted. "But the first Lord Dunstan — the one you thought looked cruel, Mandy — stepped forward and begged the king to save the fawn's life. He didn't want to lose a young animal. And as you have probably noticed, this fawn has an unusual gold blaze on her forehead. Over the years, that became a sort of trademark for our herd."

"So Lord Dunstan saved her life?" Mandy said.

"He did, but legend has it that in exchange" — Will hesitated and looked from Mandy to James — "King James was to be allowed to kill the biggest head."

"What does that mean?" James asked.

"It means the stag with the biggest antlers. Red deer stags have the biggest antlers of our native deer, so this was quite a precious trophy, even for the king," Will explained.

James frowned at the delicate creature in the tapestry. "If the fawn's a red deer, shouldn't she be called a calf?" he asked in a puzzled voice.

"Very good, James," Will said, chuckling. "You know

your stuff." James blushed as Will continued. "Strictly speaking, a young red deer is called a calf, but so many visitors call her a fawn that we do, too."

Mandy went up close to the tapestry. She could see how much work had gone into it. The horses' coats looked glossy, and their manes seemed to ripple. In the background, a man held four long-legged gray dogs on leashes. In one corner, a hedgehog was peeping out of its nest, and Mandy could see each of its spines. Red squirrels scampered along the leafy branches of the oak tree, and there was an owl peering out from a hole high up in the tree. Under the bushes in the distance were two small, long animals, but she couldn't quite make out what they were. Two more horsemen, smaller than the king, were crossing a stone bridge over a rushing stream on the far side of the clearing. A patch of ferns grew at the edge of the glade, their silvery-green fronds unfurled in the sunlight.

"The setting's very pretty. Is it a real place on the estate?" Mandy asked. James came and stood beside her, pushing his glasses up to the bridge of his nose as he studied the tapestry.

"Yes, it is," Will said. "It's in the deer park, although it doesn't look much like that now. The bridge fell down years ago. It's never been rebuilt because the river changed its course. Apparently, that's where the deer

went to drink in those days. But there's no water there at all now."

"I can hear voices," James announced, spinning around.

"Oh, dear," Will said, looking uncomfortable. "Quick, we'd better get out of here. Tilly won't be pleased if we spoil her grand entrance." He hurried across the room, pressed the switches that turned off the spotlights, and reset the tape of soft background music. Then, grabbing Mandy and James by the arm, he propelled them over to a door hidden in the paneling, opened it, and pushed them through. "Wait outside while I turn off the last switch," he told them.

Mandy and James found themselves in a dark and gloomy room. A flight of stone steps led sharply downward. The air felt damp and musty, and the walls were bare plaster.

"This is a secret passage leading to a door at the back of the house," said Will as he quietly closed the door to the tapestry room and joined them. "It's called a priest's hole. Old houses used to have them to hide priests from persecutors. I'll go first. Be careful that you don't slip."

They followed Will down the stairs, along a narrow passage that ran underneath the house, up another flight of stone steps, and out through a thick wooden door into a garden. A low redbrick wall separated the garden from the rest of the estate. The drizzle had stopped, and the sun was breaking through. In one corner of the garden stood a beech tree so old that its branches nearly touched the ground. There was a life-size statue of a deer under the tree — a proud stag with a spectacular head of antlers.

But now that Mandy had seen the tapestry, she couldn't wait to see the real thing. "Can we go and see the deer now?" she asked Will.

"Deer?" Will echoed, a blank look on his face. "What deer?"

"In the deer park," Mandy persisted. "You said that the golden blaze on the fawn in the tapestry was a common marking in your herd."

"Oh, I'm sorry," Will said apologetically. "I didn't mean to mislead you, but there haven't been deer at Cranbourne Park for a long time."

Mandy tried to hide her disappointment. "Don't you have *any* deer at all?" she asked hopefully.

"I'm afraid not." Will shook his head. "There's lots of wildlife in the woods, but no deer." Then his eyes lit up. "I'll tell you what we do have, though, if you like animals," he said. "I haven't introduced you to someone very important." He gave a long, piercing whistle.

Mandy and James waited expectantly as Will whistled again. Suddenly, Mandy saw a long streak of black and white hurtling across the lawns on the far side of the wall. The dog soared over the wall without breaking its stride and skidded to a halt at Will's feet, where it sat looking up at him, panting eagerly.

"Mandy and James, meet Lady." Will bent down and introduced them to the Dalmatian. "Lady, meet Mandy and James."

Lady lifted a paw to shake hands, first with Mandy and then James.

"She's gorgeous," Mandy said, crouching down to stroke the dog, who rolled over onto her back to have her tummy tickled.

"She's just like the Dalmatian in the painting of your dad," James observed.

"She *is* the Dalmatian in the painting of my dad," Will said, smiling.

"So, is she yours now?" Mandy asked. She scratched Lady behind the ears, making her wriggle with pleasure. Lady beat her long black-and-white tail against Mandy's legs.

"I inherited her," Will explained. "When Dad got the dog he named her Lady. My parents were divorced, and when people asked to meet the lady of the house he'd call out, 'Lady,' and she'd offer her paw to shake. My dad had a great sense of humor."

Mandy laughed. She thought she would have liked Will's dad.

"Will Lady chase a stick?" James asked, picking one up from the gravel path.

"Will she chase a stick?" Will echoed with a grin. "Just try her. She runs like the wind."

James hurled the stick into the air. It sailed over the wall, closely followed by Lady, who caught it before it had a chance to fall to the ground. She trotted back along the gravel path with it, her whole body wagging with delight, and dropped it at James's feet.

"She'll play with you for ages. You'll never tire her out," Will warned. Then he frowned and tilted his head, listening. From far away came the deep, droning sound of a motor being started.

"What's that?" Mandy asked.

"Well, along with the dog, I've also inherited all the problems that go with a stately home — and the biggest one is a new road," Will said. His voice sounded tight and angry, and his mouth was set in a grim line.

"Where is it?" asked James, puzzled. He looked around, as if he expected to see bulldozers appear at the edge of the lawn. "It won't affect you here in the park, will it?"

Will shook his head sadly. "That's where you're wrong,

James," he said. "The road is going straight through the deer park. It will devastate the forest, which has been there for hundreds of years."

Mandy was horrified. "But they can't do that!" she cried. "It's your land! You can stop them, can't you? Just say no?"

"I wish I could, Mandy, but it's a lot more complicated than that." Will crunched along the gravel path and sat down on the wall, looking out across the smooth green lawns to the edge of the forest. He began to explain. "For years, even when I was a boy, I can remember that a developer kept trying to persuade my father to sell him the land to build a road. My dad always insisted that he wouldn't allow it."

"But why does the developer want the road so badly?" James asked, sitting down next to Will.

"He owns a plot of land on the other side of the estate, and he wants to build on it," Will said. He paused, shredding a fallen leaf between his fingers. "If he does, he'll need a private access road."

"But I don't understand," Mandy protested. "How can he do that if it's *your* land? He'd need permission."

Will sighed. "It seems that just before I came back from the States my father changed his mind." His voice was pained. "I don't understand why, but he signed papers allowing the road to go ahead."

"What did your dad say about it when you saw him?" Mandy asked quietly.

"He never mentioned it. I didn't find out until after his death when I saw the family lawyer," Will said. "I had no idea what he'd done."

"Isn't there *anything* you can do?" James pressed.

"I've tried a couple of things to give myself more time, but the developer and his men always have an answer ready," Will replied. "They seem to be able to second-guess every move I make."

"Can't the lawyer do anything?" Mandy asked, feeling she was clutching at straws. She was angry at the thought of ancient woodland and all its wildlife being destroyed just to build a road.

"He checked the documents, and everything is in order," Will said tersely. "He said Dad even sealed them with his ring, so there can't be any mistake — it was Dad who authorized it. To make things even worse," he continued, standing up and brushing his trousers, "I've just been offered a herd of deer. A big house nearby is closing down, and they need to find a home for their herd. I would love to have them here. Cranbourne Park would have deer for the first time in nearly a hundred years. But we can't take them if there's a road running through the park. It wouldn't be safe." He shook his head. "Well, there's nothing I can do. I can't help them now, and it's too bad. Some of the old Cranbourne stock went into that herd."

"It just doesn't sound fair," James complained. "They shouldn't be allowed to destroy a perfectly good forest."

"And what will they do with the herd from the big house if they can't find anywhere for them?" Mandy asked cautiously, though she thought she could guess the answer.

"Understandably, the deerkeeper is doing everything possible to work something out, because he'll be out of a job, too," Will said. "But if worse comes to worse, they'll have to be practical. The herd will be slaughtered and sold to a game dealer."

"But that's terrible!" Mandy exclaimed. "We *can't* let that happen."

"It's sad, Mandy," Will agreed, "but it's a fact of life. If there's nowhere for the deer to go, how can they be kept alive?"

Three

Will let them out through a small gate in the wall, and they walked around to the front of the house. As Will stopped to straighten a sign, Mandy saw her dad outside the gift shop. She walked over to join him. James followed, his nose buried in the guidebook as he studied a map of the grounds.

"Hello, dear," Dr. Adam said when Mandy reached him. "We wondered where you'd gone."

"We skipped some of the tour, Dad," Mandy told him. She turned and motioned to Will to come over. She wanted him to be there when she told her dad about the road and the herd of deer.

"Mom's just reserving places for us in a workshop tomorrow," Mandy's dad said. "It's about old English musical instruments. I'm looking forward to trying to play a lute. Now, I wonder if I can remember the words to 'Greensleeves'?"

Mandy smiled. Her dad loved to sing, and their cottage back home often resounded with his rich, deep voice. Mandy usually teased him about his love of old-fashioned music, but today she was too preoccupied.

At that moment, Dr. Emily emerged from the shop, her hands filled with brochures and tickets. "Hello, you two!" She greeted them with a warm smile. "Why the glum faces?" She put the brochures in her bags and added, "Has Dad told you we're coming back tomorrow? I'm sure you'll find lots to do here. For a start, you missed seeing a wonderful tapestry. You'd love it, Mandy. It's full of animals!"

"We did see it, Mom. We had our own private viewing," Mandy said. She smiled as her parents looked puzzled. Just then, the crunching of footsteps across the gravel announced Will's arrival. "Mom, Dad, meet Lord Dunstan," Mandy said formally. She watched as her mom's mouth fell open slightly and her dad raised his eyebrows in surprise.

"Call me Will, please," said Will, shaking hands with

them both. "I met Mandy and James halfway through the tour. I hope you enjoyed it."

"Very much," Dr. Emily said. "Tilly is a very entertaining guide."

"Isn't she great?" Will agreed.

"We're coming back tomorrow for the workshop," Dr. Adam added. "I'm fascinated by the old instruments you have here."

"Great! I'm sure you'll enjoy it," Will said. "Dominic, the man who runs the workshop, is passionate about them. He really likes people to get involved."

"But we have something much more important than musical instruments to tell you about," Mandy interrupted. "Tell them, Will. There's a terrible problem here, Dad," she said. Beside her, James nodded seriously.

"Oh, I'm sure your folks don't want to hear about my problems," said Will, his shoulders slumping.

"What's wrong?" Dr. Adam asked, sounding concerned.

"Will's dad agreed to let a road be built right through the deer park, and Will can't stop them, and it will ruin the ancient woods, and then he can't have the deer from the other house," Mandy blurted out, hardly drawing a breath.

"Whoa, Mandy, slow down," her dad said, putting his

hands up in front of him. "One thing at a time. Now, what's this about a road?"

"This is the easiest way to explain." Will reached for James's guidebook and opened out the back cover to reveal a map of Cranbourne Park. "Right here is the deer park." He pointed to a large shaded area that represented the woodland. "On the other side is some open land that is owned by a developer. It's no use to him without an access road, and the direct way is through the park. The developer hassled my father for years, but he would never agree. Dad said the damage to the forest would be too great."

"But then he changed his mind and signed all the papers," Mandy put in.

"How strange." Dr. Emily looked thoughtful. "Still, I suppose your biggest concern now is what you can do about it."

Will nodded. "This is where the road will go, here, where this footpath is." He traced a finger right through the middle of the deer park.

"Phew," Dr. Adam said, shaking his head. "That *is* going to do a lot of damage." He gazed out at the trees. "That looks like a great example of a deciduous forest — lots of oaks, hazel, ash, and birch. I bet some of those trees are very old indeed."

"Exactly," Will agreed. "It's going to be a devastating loss."

Mandy heard a door slam and saw a man in beige pants and a green shirt locking a padlock on a wooden outbuilding to the left of the house. He turned and came toward them. When he reached the group, he nodded at the Hopes and turned to Will. "I've locked the chain saw in the toolshed," he said. Then he looked at the map in Will's hand. "I suppose you heard all the machinery arriving? They're planning to start work tomorrow."

Mandy saw a fleeting look of anguish cross Will's face, and then he composed himself.

"Let me introduce you to my estate manager," he said to the Hopes and James. "This is Gerald Bates."

Mandy looked at the manager. Mr. Bates had greasy black hair slicked back from his forehead. His face was tanned and lined from working outdoors, and his gray eyes were so pale they were almost colorless. His gaze darted around, resting on each of them in turn. Mandy glanced sideways at James, who lifted his eyebrows briefly at her.

"This is all such a shame," Dr. Emily said to the manager. "It seems awful that there's no way to stop this road from being built."

"I've done my best," Mr. Bates replied. "I was up there this morning making sure the workmen didn't trespass anywhere that they shouldn't. I won't let them get away with anything, Will, don't worry. If anyone can think of a way of stopping that road, then I'm all ears. It's not too late. We could still stop them."

"I've racked my brains, Gerald, but I'm stumped," Will admitted. "I suppose I'll just have to learn to live with the road once it's built."

"Yes, well, I'll check in on them later," Mr. Bates said, clipping the bunch of keys to his belt. "Make sure they're not taking any liberties on our land."

"Thanks, Gerald," Will said. "I'd appreciate that."

"Seems like you have a good man there," Dr. Adam said, watching the departing figure.

"Yes." Will hesitated for a moment. "I guess so."

Mandy looked at Will. He seemed as if he were miles away from them, thinking about something completely different. Then he appeared to give himself a mental shake. Turning toward Dr. Adam, he said, "Now I must leave you and get back to some work. Look around the gardens before you leave. They're lovely at this time of year. I'll see you all tomorrow."

There were many more people on the grounds now that the sun was shining. They watched Will disappear among the crowds.

"What a charming man," Dr. Emily said as they wandered around the grounds. "But what a lot he has on his shoulders."

"It's tough luck about the road," Mandy's dad agreed. "It doesn't sound as if he's going to be able to stop it. And what did you say about a herd of deer, Mandy?"

"There's another house closing down nearby. It has a herd of deer, and they've been looking for a home for them," she told her parents. "Will would have taken them here, only he can't now."

"Apparently, Cranbourne Park used to have an amazing deer herd," James chimed in. "That's what the tapestry shows — King James hunting the deer here. Will really wanted to restock the park with a new herd."

"How sad," Dr. Emily said. "It would be the obvious place for them, with all that lovely woodland to run in.

Try not to let yourself get too upset, Mandy. These things happen, and sometimes there's nothing anyone can do."

"Mom's right," her dad agreed. "You heard Will himself say that he's tried everything."

"I know," Mandy said, shoving her hands deep into her pockets. "It's just — well, it just seems so unfair."

As they made their way to the parking lot, Dr. Adam stopped and looked back at the house. "You know, I think this house would once have had a moat," he said. "Come on, we have time to have a quick look before we go home."

Mandy glanced at James and rolled her eyes in mock protest. Her dad was obviously getting carried away from looking at all that armor!

With Mandy and James on either side of him and Dr. Emily following behind, Dr. Adam strode off back to the house. "I was right!" he exclaimed when they reached the magnificent main entrance. He pointed to the ground around the house. "See that dip? That's where it's been filled in. And look, can you see here?" Dr. Adam indicated two huge iron rings on each side of the entrance. "There would have been a drawbridge here that they pulled up when they were under attack."

"And would they have poured boiling oil over the invaders?" James wondered.

"They might have done that," Dr. Adam agreed, warming to his theme. "And the attackers would have had mangonels and trebuchets and ballistae." He looked very excited at the thought.

"What are they, Dad?" Mandy demanded. "I bet you just made them up."

"I did not, Mandy Hope," her dad answered with mock indignation. "They were huge wooden contraptions, like giant catapults, that were used to hurl rocks at the walls to try to break them down."

Mandy grinned at her dad as they walked toward the parking lot again. "How did you know that, Dad?" she asked him.

"I am a positive mine of information," Dr. Adam replied loftily. "Ask me another."

Mandy thought for a moment. "Well, in the big tapestry there are two animals under a bush in the distance," she said, confident her dad would be stumped by this one. "What are they?"

"That's easy," Dr. Adam said. "A weasel and a stoat."

Mandy and James looked at each other in amazement.

"How could you tell, Dr. Adam?" James asked, sounding impressed. "I couldn't make them out at all."

At that moment Mandy noticed that her mom's shoulders were shaking as she walked in front of them. She wondered what was making her laugh.

"Well, James," Dr. Adam began, "I knew because a weasel is weasily recognized but a stoat is stoatally different."

"Oh, Dad!" Mandy sputtered as she burst out laughing. Her mom had obviously guessed what he was about to say.

The sun was just dipping down to touch the top of the distant hills when they got into the Land Rover. Mandy thought the sun looked like a great big red ball. It shimmered in a heat haze, turning the clouds orangy-yellow.

Mandy stared at it until her eyes hurt. When she looked away from the brightness and back into the car she could only make out vague shapes. "What's the real difference between a stoat and a weasel, Dad?" she asked when her eyes had readjusted.

"Ah, Mandy," Dr. Adam said. "Now, that is a tricky question."

"Not for somebody who's a mine of information!" James quipped, catching Dr. Adam's eye in the rearview mirror.

"Watch it, James," Dr. Adam said, trying to make his voice sound severe. "I don't know," he continued, turning to his wife. "Those two are pushing their luck, don't you think?"

"I do indeed, Adam," Dr. Emily agreed. "A good dose

of dishwashing is called for tonight, so they remember to have some respect for their elders."

"Elders!" Mandy laughed. "Anyway, James and I always do the dishes! But you didn't answer my question about stoats and weasels," she added, fastening her seat belt.

"Well," Dr. Adam began, "stoats are larger than weasels, with a thicker body, and they have a very distinctive black tip on their tails. Weasels are pretty tiny, with light brown fur and white underbellies. Don't be fooled by their size. They are fierce little things and can kill rabbits several times their own body weight."

Mandy thought they sounded fascinating. She made up her mind to look more closely at the tapestry tomorrow to see if she could spot the stoat's black tail.

Her dad drove slowly out of the parking lot. Along the driveway, the branches of the trees met overhead, forming a canopy that shut out the light. Mandy felt as if they were entering a dark and gloomy tunnel, and she shivered, even though the evening was warm.

As Dr. Adam slowed down to navigate a grate in the road, Mandy looked out the open window. In the half-light, trees and bushes took on strange, shadowy shapes. Mandy craned forward. She thought she could see the shape of an animal in the woods. She frowned and stared hard into the tangled undergrowth. Something was there, she was certain. And now it was coming through the bushes toward her.

Mandy felt the Land Rover shudder as its wheels crossed the metal bars of the grate. She opened her mouth to tell James what she could see, but no sound came out. Mandy continued to stare sideways out the window, transfixed by whatever it was in the woods. And then she heard the noise — the forlorn and desolate bleating of an animal in distress. It was so heartbreakingly sad that tears welled up in her eyes. Desperately, Mandy tried to shake her head to clear the tears, but she couldn't move. She could only stare into the woods and hear the sound getting closer and closer. It seemed to be following the car.

Suddenly, her eyes cleared and she saw it. Standing by the side of the driveway, staring straight at her, was a fawn. A perfect little fawn with liquid brown eyes that made Mandy's heart melt. The fawn twitched its ears, and Mandy noticed a golden blaze on its forehead. But it was the fawn's eyes that she was most drawn to. She'd never seen anything look so sad.

"What's up, Mandy?" her dad asked, turning around in his seat to look at her. "I noticed in the rearview mirror that you were staring at something."

Mandy felt as if she'd just woken up from a dream.

She hadn't even noticed that the car had stopped. To her relief, she found that she could move again. "There, look," she said urgently, twisting in her seat and pointing out the window. "Look! In the woods, there's a fawn."

But when she looked back, it had disappeared.

Four

"There *must* still be deer in the park." Mandy's voice was firm. "Wait till we tell Will. He's going to be in seventh heaven!"

"Just a minute, Mandy," Dr. Emily said cautiously. "I think that from everything we've heard today, it's out of the question that deer still live at Cranbourne Park."

"Yes, but Mom, I *saw* it," Mandy insisted. "You must have seen it, too," she said, turning to James sitting beside her.

"Well, not really." James's voice faltered slightly. His eyes looked uncertain behind his round eyeglasses.

"But it *was* a fawn!" Mandy cried out in frustration. "Trust me, I saw it clearly."

"It could have been a trick of the light, Mandy," her dad reasoned as he drove out of the entrance and onto the main road. "It was pretty dark under the trees. And don't you think that Will or Gerald would have spotted deer by now if there *were* any?"

"Dad, I know what I saw," Mandy repeated, frowning. "Honestly, it was a fawn."

"I don't think it's possible, dear," Dr. Emily said quietly but firmly. "But it's a wonderful idea, I agree, to have deer back in this ancient park." She sighed. "It's such a pity about the road."

Mandy felt frustrated as she realized she wasn't going to convince her parents. She *knew* that she had seen a fawn in the woods. She bit down hard on her bottom lip. Will would believe her.

"What's for dinner tonight?" Dr. Adam asked, changing the subject and slowing down the car.

"I haven't decided yet," Dr. Emily said. "Why?"

"There's a farm shop over there, and it's still open," Dr. Adam said, steering the car off the road and into a small parking lot. "Wait here!" he ordered.

"What's Dad doing?" Mandy asked, leaning forward and watching her dad disappear through the shop doorway.

"Don't ask me!" Dr. Emily laughed. "You know your dad. We can always rely on him to get our meals organized."

Dr. Adam emerged from the shop carrying a large cardboard box full of vegetables and fruit. He opened the back and placed the box inside. "Tonight, I am going to make us a Northumberland salad à la Hope!" he declared as he hopped back into the driver's seat and pulled away.

"That sounds like a wonderful idea, Adam," Dr. Emily said, looking around at Mandy and James in amusement and raising her eyebrows.

When they arrived at the stone cottage, Dr. Adam made straight for the kitchen while James helped Dr. Emily get the set of garden furniture from the open-sided shed beside the house. It was just light enough to eat their dinner outside. Mandy unstacked the plastic chairs and placed them around the table. Even though the sun was shining now, some of the chairs were still damp from the rain, so she went to get a cloth from the kitchen to wipe them down.

"Dad's being really secretive," Mandy told her mom when she came back. "He wouldn't let me in the kitchen."

"You know what he's like when he's being a creative chef!" Dr. Emily grinned at them both. "We'll just humor him. Mandy, would you run upstairs and bring me my book, please? I'm going to take advantage of being exiled from the kitchen and enjoy the last hour of sunshine."

"*This*," Mandy heard her dad say to himself as she went up the stairs, "is going to be the best Northumberland salad à la Hope they have ever had."

Later that evening they sat down to the biggest bowl of salad that Mandy had ever seen.

"There's everything in this, Dad." Mandy poked the salad with her fork. There were green lettuce leaves and red ones, spring onions, green beans, watercress, apples and pears, tiny sweet tomatoes, slices of crisp carrot, and shavings of Parmesan cheese. "It's fantastic!"

"Everything in this bowl was grown in Northumberland," Dr. Adam told them proudly as he gave it a final toss.

"It's really delicious, Dr. Adam," James said as he started eating his heaped plateful.

"Take some more, James." Dr. Emily pushed the bowl across to him.

Mandy leaned across and began picking out the last

few shavings of Parmesan cheese. "I didn't know Parmesan came from Northumberland, did you, James?" she asked in an innocent voice.

"No," James agreed. "I'm sure the Parmesan we have at home comes from Italy."

"That's the 'à la Hope' part," her dad replied quickly. "And for trying to be clever, you two can make Mom and me a cup of tea after you've done the dishes." He ruffled Mandy's hair and dropped the dish towel in James's lap.

While Mandy filled the sink with hot soapy water, James cleared the table. He put the remains of the salad and the bread into the fridge, humming tunelessly to himself. Mandy tucked her hair behind her ears and started to wash the plates. By the time James brought her the last dishes, she had almost finished.

"You make the tea, James, and I'll dry," she offered, taking the cloth from his shoulder. They worked in companionable silence for a few minutes before Mandy turned and looked James straight in the eye. "Tell me honestly, James," she insisted. "*Did* you see anything in the forest?"

James squared his shoulders and stared out the window, deep in thought. "I really wish I could say I saw something, Mandy," he said at last, sounding apologetic. "But I can't honestly say I did. But if *you* saw it, then it must have been there. You wouldn't make a mistake about seeing an animal."

"I did see a fawn, James, I'm absolutely certain," said Mandy, her voice firm with conviction. "There are deer in those woods. I'm sure of it."

"What did it look like?" asked James. "Was it a red deer?"

"Uh-huh." Mandy nodded. "It looked a little bigger than the one in the tapestry, but it had a golden blaze on its forehead, just like Will said when he told us about the Cranbourne deer."

"I suppose it *could* be descended from the original herd," James said thoughtfully. "I mean, it might not be that long since there were deer in the park. You know how good they are at keeping out of sight. Maybe there *are* still deer in the woods, and it's just that no one's seen them."

"Maybe it's the building work, the noise and every-thing," Mandy suggested. "Perhaps that's what's brought them out into the open."

"That's more likely to have driven them deeper into the forest!" James pointed out. "They'd be frightened."

"Will is going to be really surprised when we tell him tomorrow," Mandy said, putting the last plate away.

"Have you forgotten us?" Mandy's dad called from the yard.

"Oops!" James said guiltily, realizing he still had the empty kettle in his hand. He quickly filled it and turned it on. Mandy took out four yellow mugs decorated with pictures of chickens and placed them on a tray. While James made tea for her mom and dad, she filled the other two with cold mango juice from the fridge.

The evening was so warm they were able to sit outside until it was bedtime. Mandy was careful not to mention the deer again in front of her mom and dad. Soon she could hardly stop yawning, and she felt relieved when her mom suggested it was time for bed.

From her bedroom window, Mandy watched the big yellow moon rise. It was so clear she could make out every dip and hollow on its surface. But once she was in bed, all she could see every time she closed her eyes were the sad eyes of the fawn.

And then Mandy found herself standing back in the dark forest. She could hardly see anything. The moonlight couldn't penetrate through the thick branches and leaves of the trees. Mandy put out an arm, and a shock ran through her as her hand encountered a dewy spiderweb that clung to her fingers. An owl hooted behind her, and something scuttled through the leaves by her feet. Mandy was just beginning to make out the shapes of the trees around her when she heard a sound very close by. It was the fawn, bleating plaintively.

Mandy knew that she had to find the poor creature —
it was clearly in desperate trouble. The sound began
to fade away and Mandy tried to follow, but her legs
wouldn't work. Each time she tried to step forward her
legs turned to jelly and she fell on her knees. Pulling
herself back on her feet, she tried again, but it felt like
she was running knee-deep through sand. Her legs were
so heavy, and the fawn was moving farther away, its
pitiful cries getting fainter and fainter.

"Come back!" Mandy shouted, desperately trying to
force her body forward. "Please, come back."

And then the forest was flooded with a bright light.

"Mandy, are you having a nightmare?" Dr. Emily was
standing in the doorway, her hand on the light switch.

Mandy sat up groggily. "Oh, Mom." She groaned. "I
had a terrible dream."

"It sounded like it," her mother said in a gentle voice.
"You were calling out. That's what woke me up."

"Sorry," Mandy said. "I'm OK now."

"Sure?" Dr. Emily came across the room and smoothed
Mandy's hair back from her forehead.

"Yep, it was just a dream, that's all," Mandy said, letting her head drop back onto the pillow.

"Good night, dear," Dr. Emily said, turning off the
light and closing the door softly.

*　　*　　*

When Mandy woke the next morning, she felt full of energy. The image of the fawn was far from her mind as she sprang out of bed, pushed the window wide open, and leaned out. The sky was pale blue, with only one little wispy puff of white cloud that broke up and disappeared as Mandy watched. "It's going to be a good day," she said to herself as she brushed her teeth in the sink in the corner of her room. Pulling on shorts and a T-shirt, she danced out of the room and across the tiny landing to knock on James's door.

"Ugh?" James grunted from the depths of sleep.

"Come on, James," Mandy said encouragingly. "It's a beautiful day. We can tell Will about the deer. Maybe he'll even come with us to find her."

"Oh, right." James yawned. "OK, I'm getting up."

"Get up *now*, James," Mandy insisted. "Tell me you're up, otherwise you'll fall asleep again." She grinned as she heard the thump of feet on the floor, followed by a grumbling sound.

"I'm up now!" James called through the door. "I'll be down in a sec."

"I heard that, Mandy," Dr. Adam said as she entered the kitchen. "You bully that boy," he joked.

"It's for his own good, Dad." Mandy grinned. "He knows I mean well."

"What do you want for breakfast?" Dr. Adam asked.

"There's toast, yogurt, or cereal, though we're a little short of milk."

"Mom's got some long-life stuff in this cupboard," Mandy told him, reaching up to get it. "But I want yogurt. I'm not that hungry." She smiled at her dad as she handed him the carton of milk. "Especially after eating most of the salad in Northumberland last night!"

"It was good, wasn't it?" Dr. Adam said, looking pleased. "But what's this I heard you saying to James about deer?"

Mandy hesitated. She wasn't sure her dad would want to know that she still believed she had seen a fawn in the woods. "I . . . we . . . want to tell Will about seeing the deer last night," she told him.

Dr. Adam's voice was cautious. "Mandy, dear, I don't think you should make too much of this. I know you're sure you saw a deer, but I really don't think that you could have. They couldn't have stayed hidden all this time. Tilly told us it's about a hundred years since deer were last seen at Cranbourne."

"That may be true, Dad, but I did see a deer," Mandy insisted.

Dr. Adam shrugged. "Look, here come Mom and James. Why don't we have our breakfast in the yard?"

"Good idea," Dr. Emily said. She opened the back door and stepped outside. "It's pretty warm already."

"Look at that view!" Dr. Adam said as he poured himself another cup of coffee. The cottage was halfway up a hill, and below them stretched rolling countryside dotted here and there with tall green trees. It was so quiet they could hear the splashing of a small river that wound its way alongside the bottom of the valley.

"There's a hawk," said James, pointing to a large bird sitting motionless on a branch below them. As he spoke, the bird took off and soared majestically into the blue sky.

"I wonder if it's spotted a mouse," Mandy said, watching the bird as it folded its wings and plunged dramatically toward the ground. Just when she thought it couldn't possibly stop in time, the bird opened its wings and swooped upward again. Its beak was empty.

"Oh, well," said Mandy. "Better luck next time." She scraped out the last spoonful of yogurt and pushed back her chair, looking at her watch. Her stomach felt tight with anxiety. She was eager to get to Cranbourne Park to tell Will about the fawn, but she didn't want to hurry her parents. She knew they were convinced she'd made a mistake.

By the time they pulled into the parking lot, Cranbourne Park was getting busy. Several people were lined up to buy tickets for the workshop. Dr. Emily and Dr. Adam already had their tickets so they went straight into the house, following the directions to the workshop, which was in the library on the ground floor. Mandy and James went searching for Will.

"Aren't you two doing the workshop?" Tilly asked when they poked their heads into the shop.

"No," Mandy replied, shaking her head. "But we have some important news for Will."

Tilly looked at her watch. "You'll probably find him in the office," she suggested. "Go around the side of the house and across the courtyard. It's the door right in front of you."

Mandy and James raced off. As they crossed the shady cobblestone courtyard, they could see Will through the window, tapping numbers into a calculator. "Come in," he mouthed, beckoning.

Mandy pushed the door open and found Lady waiting on the other side. She fussed over the dog as they sat down opposite Will. The office was large, lined with shelves full of files and papers. There were two desks, and Will sat at the larger one. Behind him, Mandy could see an open door leading to another room with yet more shelves and several big filing cabinets.

"Good morning!" Will greeted them with a smile, although Mandy thought he looked pale and tired. "What can I do for you?"

"We have some news for you," James said, looking at Mandy.

Will leaned back in his chair, crossed his arms, and raised his eyebrows at them. "OK, shoot," he said.

"Last night," Mandy began, "as we went down the driveway, I saw a fawn in the woods!"

"What?" Will sat up sharply. "Mandy, that's just not possible."

"But I *did* see it, really I did," Mandy insisted. "And

James almost saw it, too." She looked at James for support. He nodded encouragingly. It was obvious that he believed her.

"Listen," said Will, "there's no way deer could be at Cranbourne without anyone knowing about it. I mean, there would be evidence. You know the sort of thing, hoofprints and droppings. And there would be a browse line in the woods, where the deer have eaten all the leaves off the trees as far up as they can reach."

"Honestly, Will, I'm certain," Mandy promised him. "I looked right into its eyes."

Will got up and walked restlessly across the floor. "I can tell you feel sure, Mandy," he said. "But I have to say I think you're mistaken." He looked apologetic when he saw the disappointed expression on Mandy's face. "I'm really sorry, but I'm afraid it's just not possible." He stopped at the sound of footsteps outside the open window.

Mandy glanced out the window and saw Gerald Bates crossing the courtyard.

"Gerald!" Will called from the doorway. "A minute of your time, please." He walked back to his seat behind the desk. "Gerald knows the estate better than anyone," he explained to Mandy and James. "He'd certainly know if there were any deer around."

The estate manager strolled into the office, nodding to Mandy and James. "What's the problem?" he said to Will.

"Mandy thinks she saw a deer in the woods last night — a fawn," Will said, looking over at Mandy, who nodded eagerly. "What do you think?"

"Not a chance," Mr. Bates said immediately. "You didn't see any flying pigs as well, did you?" he teased, his lips curving into a thin smile.

"Of course not," Mandy retorted, feeling herself turning red. "Just the fawn."

Ignoring Mandy, Gerald Bates turned back to Will. "You shouldn't let kids wander around in the deer park," he said irritably. "It's much too dangerous with all the road machinery. There could be a bad accident, and then what would happen?"

Mandy saw Will blush. "They were in a car at the time, actually," he told the manager in a cold voice. "And unless I'm mistaken, the work hasn't started yet."

"Yes, well, I was only thinking of the estate's responsibilities," Mr. Bates said grudgingly. "The builders will be starting this morning, and we should make the deer park out of bounds to the public."

"Yes, perhaps you're right." Will looked thoughtful. "But not all of it. The deer park is pretty big, and the road isn't going to affect *all* of it, is it?"

"Well, it's your decision." Gerald Bates shrugged. "If you want to take the risk of an accident.... Now, if there's nothing more," he added, his voice brisk, "I'll get on with my work." Turning swiftly, he marched out of the room.

Will watched Mr. Bates walk across the courtyard and through a small side gate that led to the garden. Then he reached for a pile of papers and said, "Sorry, Mandy, but your fawn must have been a trick of the light." He sounded genuinely sorry, and Mandy was relieved that at least Will hadn't laughed at her like Gerald had.

"That's all right," Mandy said calmly. She was becoming resigned to the fact that nobody believed her. "We'd better go." She could see that Will had a mountain of paperwork.

"Catch you later," Will called after them. "Have a good day."

Outside, James gave Mandy a sideways look as she halfheartedly kicked a stone across the courtyard. "What do we do now?" he asked.

"I don't know," Mandy replied with a sigh. "I sort of hoped we'd go looking for deer with Will this morning." She shrugged her shoulders. "Do you have any ideas? I don't really want to go to the music workshop."

"Why don't we look for the place that's pictured in

the tapestry?" James suggested. "You know, where the fawn's life was saved? It looked like a pretty amazing spot."

"That might be fun." Mandy's eyes lit up, and she felt much more cheerful. "Hang on, though. How will we find it?"

"We could look for the ruins of the bridge," James said. "Tilly can tell us which way to go."

They hurried to the shop, where they found Tilly tidying the containers of Cranbourne Park pencils and bookmarks, which stood next to the cash register. There were no tours while the music workshop was on, so she was helping in the gift shop for the day.

When they had revealed their plans, Tilly looked encouraging. "The trail is very overgrown, but you should be able to find it," she told them, showing them the direction on the map in the guidebook. "There's a postcard of the tapestry here. You can take it with you for reference."

"Thanks," said Mandy. "That will be really helpful." She looked at Tilly thoughtfully. "We saw Mr. Bates just now. He seemed really angry when we started talking about the deer that" — James nudged Mandy in the ribs, as if to remind her to be careful about what she said — "used to live in the woods," she finished.

"Did he?" Tilly mused. Lowering her voice, she confided, "I have to admit, I'm not sure about that man. Once I went into old Lord Dunstan's office and found his lordship asleep in his chair. I couldn't wake him up, and I got really worried. Then, suddenly, Gerald came out from the back room with some papers. I can't prove anything, but I'm sure he was up to no good."

Mandy was shocked. "What did Will say about it?" she asked.

"Will hadn't returned home yet," Tilly admitted, opening a deep drawer and taking out a stack of cards wrapped in cellophane. "And when he did get back, I didn't really want to tell him what I'd seen. He was worried enough with his dad being ill. Anyway, you'd better be getting along now or you won't be back in time for lunch. And don't worry about what I said about Gerald Bates. I'm probably being oversensitive. It's just that the park means so much to me, I almost feel like part of the family. Now, off you go, and have a good morning!"

"Thanks, Tilly. If we're not back before the workshop ends, could you tell my parents where we went?" Mandy asked her.

"Will do," Tilly agreed.

Full of excitement now that they had something definite to do, Mandy and James followed the signs to the deer park. They found the footpath easily — the one that Will had said would be swallowed up by the new road. But as they moved deeper into the woods, the trail became narrower and very overgrown. Mandy stopped abruptly when she was confronted with a huge patch of brambles across the path. Behind her, James tripped over a tree root and barreled into her, knocking her forward.

"James!" Mandy exclaimed as the brambles scratched her bare legs. "I wish I hadn't put on shorts this morning."

"Sorry," James said sheepishly. "I wasn't looking."

"We'll have to make a detour around this," Mandy decided, rubbing her legs and looking for another route.

"I see what Will means about the deer park being empty," James said as they stepped into the undergrowth to navigate their way around the bramble patch.

Mandy had to agree. "There certainly haven't been deer browsing around here," she said with a wry smile at James as he ducked under a perilously low branch.

Soon they had made so many detours that they'd lost the original trail. Mandy felt sure that they were going in circles. Then, just when she was beginning to think they'd never find the place in the tapestry, Mandy pushed her way out from among the trees and into a broad clearing. "Look, James," she said breathlessly. "I think we've found it."

The forest around them was so dense that the clearing was like an airy cavern among the dark trees. The branches almost met overhead, and the ground was covered with soft, light-green grass. In the middle was a huge, dead tree. Its leafless boughs forked crookedly upward toward the leafy canopy. Through a gaping split in its side, they could see the vast hollow interior.

"This must be the oak tree," James said as he walked around the enormous blackened trunk. "It looks as though it's been struck by lightning." He took the postcard out of his pocket and held it up, looking critically from the card to the tree and back again. "The bridge should be behind it, over there," he said at last.

"Here are some stones!" Mandy cried, running across the glade to an uneven pile of gray rocks. "Come over here and look, James! There's some carving on this one." She scraped the moss away from the smooth square stone to reveal an intricate shape.

"That's the Dunstan crest!" James exclaimed. "A stag's head and a sword."

"The same as on Will's ring," Mandy agreed.

"This is definitely it, Mandy," James decided, studying the postcard again. "That dip in the ground is where the old riverbed was. This is where King James's horse would have been standing." He walked over and stood at the edge of the ancient river.

Mandy stood beside the dead oak tree. "And Lord Dunstan would have been here," she said.

"So the fawn would have been behind you. Look —"
James stopped speaking and came to stand beside
Mandy with the postcard. He frowned and looked down
at the card.

As Mandy waited for James to continue, she heard
a rustling sound coming from the bushes at the side
of the glade. James's head shot up. He'd heard it, too.
As one they turned. Mandy's eyes grew wide, and she
gasped. Standing in front of them, less than three yards
away, was the fawn.

Five

Mandy felt the air around them shiver. She stared at the fawn. It met her gaze with its piercing dark eyes. On its forehead was a bright golden blaze. Then she looked around and felt her heart skip a beat.

The glade looked completely different. The burned oak tree was a towering, living oak tree again, majestic and proud, its branches rustling with thick green leaves. Behind it, the little stone bridge was in one piece, with a stream sparkling beneath it.

Mandy felt the back of her neck begin to tingle, and a shiver ran down her spine. What was happening? Then,

in the distance, a hunting horn sounded, very faint and far away.

Mandy could feel the fawn watching them steadily. She turned her head and returned the fawn's gaze. It was as if the fawn were desperately trying to tell her something.

Then, rhythmically and methodically, the fawn began to paw at the ground with its hoof. Mandy watched, spellbound. After some moments, the fawn stopped. The grass around its legs seemed to quiver in the breeze.

The clearing was eerily silent, except for the gentle rustling of leaves in the treetops. Once again the fawn began to scrape at the patch of grass. Then it lifted its beautiful head and stared at Mandy for what seemed like minutes before turning away.

Mandy felt as if the air were shivering again, and she glanced anxiously at James. He was shaking his head as if he were just coming up from underwater. When Mandy looked back, the fawn had gone.

She stared around her. The clearing was just as they had found it. The oak tree was blackened and dead, the bridge nothing but a pile of stones.

"Mandy," James whispered, "what do you think happened just now?"

"I don't know," Mandy said slowly. She felt as if she

had just woken up from a vivid dream. "But, James, it was the same fawn I saw last night. I *knew* I'd seen it!"

"This is really weird!" James said. "Everything looked like the scene in the tapestry. We didn't imagine all that, did we? Do you — do you think we went back in time?" His voice sounded strained and incredulous, as if he couldn't quite believe what he was saying.

"No, we didn't imagine it," Mandy agreed. "I felt the air sort of wobble, and then everything changed. But the fawn was there, too." She stared across the clearing to where the creature had been standing. "Maybe it's not that strange that no one else can see the fawn." She turned to James, her eyes wide with excitement. "James, do you think the fawn is a *ghost*?"

James looked taken aback, then he nodded slowly. "You could be right," he said. "The fawn that the king didn't kill. And just now, we went back to the fawn's time. But why?"

Mandy frowned, picturing again the desperate look in the fawn's limpid eyes. "Do you think she wants us to do something?" she said.

"Maybe. She seemed to want to show us something on the ground over there," James commented. He walked across the glade and peered down at the grass. "Hey, look!" he exclaimed. "There's a tiny fern growing down here. And it looks like —" Just to make absolutely certain, he pulled the postcard of the tapestry out of his pocket. "It's the same!" he cried excitedly. "Look, Mandy, it's definitely the same as the fern in the tapestry."

Mandy took the postcard from him and studied it. "But so what?" she said. "It probably grows all over the place."

But before James could answer, a loud, rumbling roar came from close by. Mandy felt her heart start to pound. She guessed it was the bulldozers starting up. They were beginning to build the road.

Six

Mandy looked at her watch. It was nearly two o'clock. "James, we'd better get back," she said. "I didn't realize we'd been away so long."

"What happened in the clearing was kind of scary, Mandy," James admitted as they walked back through the woods. "Do you think it might happen again? Everything changing like that?"

"I suppose it could. I didn't exactly feel scared, but I know what you mean," Mandy agreed.

"Should we tell Will, or your mom and dad?" James asked.

"Maybe we shouldn't say anything yet," Mandy suggested. Even though she now thought Will was probably right about there being no live deer in the park, she didn't think he would be very pleased to hear Mandy say she was sure the fawn was a ghost!

"They probably wouldn't believe us, anyway," James said.

As they neared the house, the noise of the machines grew louder. Mandy felt angry as she thought of all the ancient trees and their wildlife being churned up.

But as they walked past the house, Mandy couldn't help smiling when she heard her father's voice wafting on the air through an open window.

"Alas, my love, you do me wrong,
To cast me out discourteously."

She grinned at James, and they went over to the window and peeked in. There were a lot of people in the room. A group of men and women, some of them wearing old-fashioned robes, were playing stringed instruments that looked like pear-shaped guitars. James whispered that they were lutes. Dr. Adam had his back to them as he held a sheet of music and continued to sing loudly. Dr. Emily sat on the other side of the room, facing the window.

Mandy waited until her mom saw them and smiled,

then she led James off in search of some lunch. Some-how, everything seemed more normal now.

"You were gone a long time," Tilly said when they walked into the shop. "You've missed lunch, but your mom put a couple of rolls aside for you." She reached under the counter and took out a tray with the wrapped rolls and two small bottles of fresh orange juice on it. Mandy carried it outside, and they found a seat and ate their lunch in the warm afternoon sun. It was blissfully peaceful. Only birdsong or the occasional melody drift-ing out from the music workshop broke the silence.

"What do you want to do now?" James asked as he put the wrappings and empty bottles into a trash can.

"Let's ask Tilly where Will is," Mandy suggested, jump-ing up. "We can find out what's happening about the road." They made their way back along the gravel path and into the gift shop, where it felt pleasantly cool after the bright sunshine.

"Let me think," Tilly said. "If he's not in the office, then he'll be in the tapestry room. Some of the bulbs in the spotlights burned out this morning. He promised to replace them."

Mandy and James walked through the restaurant and across the courtyard to the office. It was deserted. They followed the signs to the tapestry room on the first floor of the house and knocked loudly on the closed door.

"Come in!" Will's voice called. "It's open."

Mandy pushed the door open. Will was standing at the top of a very tall ladder, screwing a bulb into a recess in the ceiling. "Good," he said when he saw them. "You can help me test these. There are some switches beside the door. Three of them are off. Could you flick them on, please?"

James flicked the switches, and the spots in the ceiling immediately lit up.

"Great, thanks," Will said, climbing down. He folded the ladder, carried it across the room, and leaned it against the wall. As he was walking back to the door, he glanced at the tapestry. He stopped dead and stared hard at it for a long time. "It *can't* be," Mandy heard him say under his breath.

Then Will turned to them, running his hand through his hair. Mandy thought he looked even more pale and tired than before. "I must be going crazy!" he said with a short laugh. "It's just that I thought — no, it must be my imagination."

"Is something wrong?" Mandy asked, puzzled.

"Come and see for yourselves," Will said, motioning them over to the tapestry. "It's the fawn. I know it sounds ridiculous, but I think it's *moved*."

Mandy felt a thrill run through her. She and James walked up to the tapestry for a closer look. James took out the postcard, which was beginning to look battered, and held it up so they could compare it with the tapestry in front of them.

Mandy felt stunned. The fawn in the tapestry was no longer standing on the patch of earth. It *had* moved. Now it was at the edge of the glade, closer to the trees. Its hooves were hidden by the delicate green fronds of ferns.

Mandy took a deep breath. "The fawn *has* moved," she told Will. Before he could say anything, she continued. "But we have something even stranger to tell you."

"Go on," Will said curiously. "I'm all ears."

"Well," Mandy began, "you remember I told you I'd seen the fawn in the woods?" She paused. "This morning we saw it again. Both of us." Mandy looked at James, who nodded in agreement. "We went into the woods, looking for the place in the tapestry. We found the clearing, and then something happened. Everything sort of changed, as if we'd gone back in time."

Will frowned. "What on earth do you mean, Mandy?" he asked.

"Well, the oak tree was like that." Mandy pointed at the magnificent tree pictured in the tapestry.

"And the bridge was there, over the river," James said, helping out. "And one of the stones had the Dun-

stan crest on it. And the fawn looked just like that one."
He pointed.

"But I don't understand," Will began.

Mandy shrugged. "We don't, either, but it really did
happen, I promise."

"And like in the tapestry now," James added, "the
fawn wasn't standing on a patch of earth, it was standing among some ferns."

Will looked at him sharply. "What sort of ferns?" he
asked.

"The same as these." James waved his hand toward the
pale green fronds curling around the fawn's slender legs.

Will's eyes lit up. He fired questions at them. "Are you
sure? Absolutely? Could you find it again?"

Mandy felt confused. "Why are you so concerned
about the ferns?" she asked him.

"Well, if that really *is* the same kind of fern as in the
tapestry, then it's *incredibly* rare." Will looked rather
stunned. "Everyone thinks it's been extinct for years. If
there's some left, it would be a protected species."

"The road!" Mandy gasped as the importance of the
ferns dawned on her. "They won't be able to put it in!"
she said.

"Nope!" Will pushed open the door to the corridor.
"Come on, let's go and phone Plantlife."

With Mandy and James in hot pursuit, Will hurried along the corridor and down the back stairs to the office. When they reached the office he sat at the smaller desk and pulled the telephone toward him. "Now, where's that number?" he muttered under his breath, riffling through a big black leather book. "Here we are!"

"What's Plantlife?" James asked as Will punched the number into the phone.

Will covered the mouthpiece with his hand. "It's a wild plant conservation charity," he explained. "They have a program called Back from the Brink that rescues endangered species. They'll tell us what to do next."

Mandy looked over at James as Will began speaking on the phone. Now she felt sure that the fawn they had seen in the clearing was the ghost of the tapestry fawn. She remembered what Will had told them about the fawn — she was a young doe who had been saved from the king's arrow by the first Lord Dunstan. Was that why she wanted to come back and help now?

Mandy and James waited quietly, listening to Will. They nearly jumped out of their skin when Gerald Bates emerged from the back room behind them. They hadn't realized he was in there.

"Good news?" he asked, raising his eyebrows at them.

Mandy nodded. "Very good, actually," she said proudly.

"James and I have found an endangered fern. Will thinks it might be enough to stop the road."

"He's talking to Plantlife now," James added.

"Oh, is he?" Mr. Bates said. "And where is the fern?"

"Up by the dead oak tree, where the bridge used to be," Mandy told the manager. Then she looked back at Will, trying to work out what was being arranged for the ferns.

"That's fine!" Will was saying. "First thing in the morning, then. Yes, I'll be here. Good-bye." He replaced the receiver and looked up at them. "They're sending a botanist down tomorrow. The man I spoke to was really excited about the ferns," he added, sounding hopeful.

"I'd better go and stop the bulldozers," Gerald Bates said urgently. "We don't want them going in that direction."

"Good thinking, Gerald," said Will. He smiled at Mandy and James. "Why don't you two show me where you saw the ferns?"

"Sure," Mandy agreed. "But could we have another look at the tapestry first?" She wanted to check something out.

"Of course," said Will. He stood up and led the way out of the office and across the courtyard to the house.

As they walked up the back stairs, James glanced at

Mandy and raised his eyebrows, as if to ask what she was doing.

"Wait and see," Mandy whispered to him.

When they reached the room at the end of the hall, Mandy, James, and Will stood in front of the tapestry, hardly able to believe their eyes.

Will let out a low whistle. "Well, would you believe it?" he said, staring at the fawn.

"It's moved again," said Mandy softly, looking into the fawn's dark brown eyes. The fawn was no longer standing in the ferns at the edge of the clearing. Instead, it was back on the patch of bare earth beside the oak tree.

James nodded in understanding. "The tapestry fawn wanted to show us the ferns as well," he said quietly. "It *must* be the same one we saw in the woods."

Mandy glanced sideways at Will, who was still gazing at the tapestry. Did he think they had seen the ghost of the fawn? Somehow, it didn't seem important now that they had found out about the ferns.

Just then, Will caught Mandy's eye and smiled. "Come on," he said. "Let's go and find this rare fern." He waited until Mandy and James were in the hallway, then he switched off the lights and closed the door firmly.

They walked through the house and down the front steps. Outside the restaurant, several people were milling around, talking and laughing. Mandy spotted her parents and ran over to them.

"We're having a wonderful day, Mandy," Dr. Adam declared when he saw her. "I've even tried playing a lute."

"It's all truly fascinating," Dr. Emily told Will as he joined them. "You were right, Dominic does know his stuff."

"I'm glad you're enjoying it," Will said politely.

"What about *our* news?" Mandy was almost jumping with excitement. She could hardly wait to tell her mom and dad about the ferns.

"What on earth is it, Mandy?" Dr. Emily looked worried. "Everything's all right, isn't it?"

"Everything's great!" Mandy's eyes shone. "James and I found some ferns that belong to a protected species, and it's going to stop the road."

"Is that true?" Dr. Adam asked Will. "That's wonderful news."

"Well, it's not definite yet," Will said. "But if we're right about the ferns, I'm sure we'll be able to call off the road."

"Well, you two are great!" Mandy's dad said, squeezing Mandy's arm and patting James on the shoulder. "Will you join us for tea?" he asked Will. "I'd like to hear all about it."

"We're taking Will to show him where we found them," Mandy said.

"Maybe we could get together after your next music session," Will suggested. "We shouldn't be gone very long."

"Of course," said Dr. Adam. "Good luck!" He waved to them as they crunched across the gravel toward the path that led into the woods.

Will knew the site of the old bridge, and he took them along a much shorter route than before, without needing to make complicated detours to avoid bramble bushes.

"Perhaps we should have brought some wire to put around the ferns," James said thoughtfully as they walked through the trees. "Because it's so important, I mean."

"I think it ought to be pretty safe," Will assured him. "It's not as if anyone comes up here. The deer park is open to the public, but most of the trails are so overgrown that people never venture very far from the house."

As they drew closer to the clearing, Mandy began to feel excited. She walked faster and was soon ahead of the others. But when she reached the edge of the clearing, fear and dismay shot through her, and she groaned out loud. She waited, utterly dejected, for the others to join her.

"Oh, no!" Will said miserably as he stopped beside her. "It looks like Gerald couldn't stop them in time."

The clearing was hardly recognizable. The blackened oak tree had been pushed over and lay splintered and crushed on the earth. A few slender saplings lay up-rooted and scattered around it, their green leaves already turning limp and dry. The stones from the ruined bridge were barely visible, they had been pressed so deeply into the soil by heavy tires.

Mandy stared in horror at the twin tracks in the earth. How could the people driving the machines bear to cause so much destruction? She watched James's shoulders

sag as he walked over to where they had seen the ferns. Gently he stroked his hand over the churned-up earth. Mandy could see despair in his eyes when he looked over at them.

"Nothing," James said bitterly. "They're all gone."

Seven

"Come on," Will said heavily. He sounded defeated and resigned. "Let's go back. There's nothing to be done here."

"But how did the bulldozers get this far so quickly?" Mandy protested. "I thought they'd just started."

"So did I," said Will. "They must be working on a really tight schedule. Probably to give me less time to find a way to stop them!"

With heavy hearts they started back to the house along the path that Mandy and James had taken the day before. It soon became clear that the road builders had made spectacular progress. The machines had cut a wide swath through the forest, and the churned-up earth looked bare and ugly. Even where they had managed to steer between trees, the huge machines had knocked off branches and leaves as they passed, leaving a messy green trail of destruction.

"They must be working flat out," Will muttered. He paused as they reached the edge of the lawn and looked back into the woods. All was dark and silent there now, except for the rustling of leaves in the breeze. It was hard to believe so much damage had been caused in one afternoon.

"It's still not too late to stop the road, Will," Mandy said, trying hard to be positive. "We'll have to find another way."

"I wish I had your confidence, Mandy," Will said sadly. "I'd better go and phone the guy from Plantlife and tell him what's happened. I'll catch up with you later." He jogged off toward the house and disappeared around the side, heading for the office.

"I wonder what happened to the fawn," Mandy said as she and James walked across the lawn. Faint singing drifted out of an open window on the ground floor. The music workshop was under way again. "In the end, I mean," Mandy went on. "I hope she just died of old age."

"What about the stag?" James said. "I wonder if King James ever *did* get the biggest pair of antlers."

"It didn't say anything in the guidebook," Mandy told him. "I looked."

"We could ask Will," James suggested.

"I don't think we should bother him," Mandy decided. "Let's go and ask Tilly." She turned right and headed for the courtyard. Tilly was inside the gift shop, sitting on a stool behind the counter and reading a book.

"Hi, Tilly!" said Mandy as they entered. She decided not to tell Tilly about the destruction of the ferns as she wasn't sure if Will had told her about their discovery in the first place. "James and I have been wondering — do you know what happened after the scene in the tapestry? Did King James get his antlers?"

"Well, I don't know if it was King James, but somebody did!" Tilly said with a smile. "They're hanging in the Great Hall now. Didn't you see them on the tour?"

"We missed some of the tour," Mandy reminded her. "When we met Will."

"Of course you did," said Tilly. She looked around the empty shop. "Come on, I'll lock up for a few minutes and take you over."

She took a BACK IN FIVE MINUTES sign from underneath the counter and propped it in the window. Unhooking a hefty bunch of keys from her belt, she locked the door behind them. "Follow me," she said. "But we'd better be quick."

Mandy and James followed Tilly over to the main entrance. She led them into an enormous oak-paneled room whose ceiling reached right up to the roof. "There," she said, waving her arm dramatically.

Mandy gasped. Perched above the cavernous fireplace was the biggest pair of antlers she had ever seen.

"Wow!" James exclaimed. "Can you imagine what the stag would have looked like?"

"A very impressive animal," Tilly agreed. "But you know, I don't know exactly who killed him. Let's go down to the archives and have a look. It's all useful information for my tour."

Mandy and James followed her back out of the Great Hall, down a long, stone-flagged corridor, and then down a very narrow set of stairs. Mandy realized they must be in the basement.

"Here we are." Tilly stopped in front of a steel-paneled door and inserted a key into the lock. "Help me push, please. It's a fireproof door, and it's really heavy."

The three of them put their shoulders to the door and pushed. Slowly, it creaked open. Tilly switched on the lights, revealing a windowless room full of dark wooden cabinets. Some of them looked very old. Each cabinet held half a dozen drawers, and on the front of each drawer was a handwritten list of dates.

"These are the estate records that the manager keeps. As you can see, Cranbourne's had some very conscientious recordkeepers!" Tilly gestured to the rows of cabinets and laughed. "OK, let's think," she said. "King James was here around 1610, I believe. Look for a date around that time."

"Here it is." James found it on the first label he examined. "Cranbourne Park 1590–1690. It must be in here." He tugged at the drawer, but it was locked.

Tilly shuffled through her bunch of keys until she found a small brass key. She unlocked the drawer and pulled it open to reveal a shallow stack of big leather-covered books.

"Let's try this one," she said, taking out a book and handing it to Mandy. It was surprisingly heavy. "This says it covers 1600 onward." Tilly took a pair of white cotton gloves from the top of the cabinet and put them on. "We have to be careful how we handle these. They're very old and precious." She laid the book on a table and carefully opened it. The leather cover crackled as if it hadn't been opened in years. Tilly leafed slowly through the yellowed pages, which were covered with lines of tiny, looped handwriting.

At first, Mandy and James could hardly read the strange

writing, and Tilly had to read it out loud. But after a few minutes they began to get the hang of it. It wasn't long before they found what they were looking for.

"*. . . in the year Sixteen Hundred and Eleven in the month of September by the Hollow Pond King James did with a single arrow kill the biggest head of the Cranbourne herd of red deer. The stag's antlers had more than twenty tines.*"

"Oh," Mandy sighed. "Somehow it seems sad, even though it was a long time ago."

"It does, doesn't it?" Tilly agreed. "Poor old thing."

"What's a tine?" James asked, reading the report again.

"The tines are the points of the antlers," Tilly explained. "Each point counts as one tine. The more points, the bigger the stag."

"So is twenty tines a lot?" Mandy asked.

Tilly nodded. "I'll say! Nowadays, a royal is a twelve-pointer, and that's considered a lot. That herd must have been well looked after. Antler size is directly related to feeding."

"How come you know so much about deer?" James asked.

Tilly shut the book and placed it back in the drawer. "I thought you might ask that." She laughed. "My brother works on an estate in the Scottish Highlands. Now, I must get back to the shop." She locked the drawer again and led the way out of the basement room.

"Where's Hollow Pond?" James asked as they walked back along the stone passage to the Great Hall.

"I was trying to think of that myself, James," Tilly confessed. "As far as I know, there's only one pond on the estate, and it's not called Hollow Pond."

"It seems a shame that the stag had to be killed at all," Mandy said. "Even if it was to save the fawn."

"In the tapestry, you mean?" Tilly said. She slowed down and turned to Mandy. "It wouldn't have been so unusual, I don't think. After all, an old stag will eventually be overthrown by a stronger, younger stag, but a breeding female can keep the herd going for a long time." She gasped as they rounded the corner of the house and the entrance to the gift shop came in sight. "Oh, my goodness, look at that line." Apologizing to the waiting people, Tilly quickly unlocked the door and went behind the counter. She waved good-bye to Mandy and James before she started to help the first customer.

"Let's see if we can find the pond," Mandy suggested. She glanced at her watch. There was still another hour before the music workshop finished.

"OK. If there's only one pond, it should be on that

map." James pointed to a laminated map on a wooden display board just outside the shop. They stood in front of it and searched for the location of the pond.

"Here it is!" Mandy cried, standing on tiptoe. "Look, if you follow this brook near the driveway, it leads to it. But it's not called Hollow. It's called Tagfell Pond." She looked around at James. "That sounds odd."

"Wait a minute," James said, craning to see better. "No, it's not. The *s* has worn off. It's called Stagfell!" he exclaimed. "It has to be the place, doesn't it?"

Mandy nodded. "Maybe they named the pond after the stag," she said.

"That would make sense," James agreed. "Let's go and have a look." He studied the map for a moment, running his finger along a faint blue line that led from just in front of the house to the pond.

"OK," said Mandy. "It looks like we can follow the stream all the way."

They walked across the lawn to where a narrow stream ran under the driveway.

"Look, Stagfell Pond," James said, pointing to a wooden sign affixed to a tree.

They walked beside the stream, following it along the edge of the forest, where the trees thinned out into a broad meadow. It was very peaceful, and the house was soon out of sight. The ground started to rise steeply, and the stream disappeared into a dark tunnel underground.

"Let's go over that ridge," James said. "I bet the pond is on the other side." He climbed up the short slope, then turned and gave Mandy a hand up. From the top of the ridge they looked down on Stagfell Pond. It was much bigger than they had expected and obviously very deep, because the water looked almost black and as still as glass.

"Let's walk around it," Mandy suggested. "There might be a plaque or something saying where the stag was killed." She ran down the slope and set off around the pond on a narrow path that took them a little way into the woods. "This is such a pretty forest," Mandy said sadly, looking at the ancient, moss-covered trees. "How can anyone want to spoil it with a horrible road?"

"I wish people would just leave things alone," James agreed angrily.

"Especially places where animals live." Mandy lowered her voice. "James, do you think we might see the fawn again?"

"I don't know," James replied. "It's already shown us the ferns. I don't know what else it could do."

"I wish there was something else *we* could do to stop

the road and save the forest," Mandy said. "That poor fawn. I'm sure it wants the other herd of deer to come here, the ones Will said would be homeless."

"It would be a great place for them," James admitted. "Without the road, that is!"

"But time's running out, James. If we don't stop the road soon, it will be too late!" Mandy pointed out. "If only we could think of something."

"I know," James agreed. He looked at his watch. "Time is running out for us, too, Mandy — only half an hour left."

Suddenly, Mandy grabbed James's arm and pulled him to a standstill.

James followed her gaze and saw that the bushes beside the pond were starting to shake and rustle, even though there was no wind. "What do you think it is?" he whispered.

Mandy shook her head, but before she could say anything a loud, defiant bellowing filled the air. She put her hands over her ears and saw James do the same. Now the bushes were shaking so violently that Mandy began to feel nervous.

As abruptly as it had started, the roaring stopped and the bushes stopped shaking. All Mandy could hear was the whispering of leaves in the trees. She felt as if she were rooted to the spot. And then a shiver ran through her body. Standing in the bushes, his noble head held high, was an enormous stag.

The stag stood motionless for a moment. Then he gazed around, slowly turning his magnificent set of antlers toward them. He began to walk forward with dignified, measured steps.

Mandy hardly dared to breathe as he approached. She could see his huge muscles rippling under his rich red coat. The stag came closer and closer. To Mandy's alarm, it looked as if the stag was going to walk between her and James. She was convinced that he would knock them off their feet with his antlers.

As the stag stepped between them, Mandy thrust out her hands to push away the antlers. But there was nothing there. She let her hands fall back to her sides.

The stag walked away from the edge of the pond, farther into the trees. Then he stopped and waited, turning his head and staring back at them. The expression in the stag's eyes was so sad that Mandy felt her heart ache. The power of his gaze seemed almost to pull her off her feet, and, as if she had no choice, she began to walk toward him.

As soon as she drew near, the stag backed away. Mandy put out her hand and beckoned urgently to James. Somehow, she knew they had to follow the stag. The magnificent creature led them farther into the forest, away from the pond and down the path cleared by the bull-dozers.

"Where is he taking us?" James whispered to Mandy.

"I don't know," Mandy admitted. "But have you ever seen such sad eyes? They sort of pulled me toward him."

"I know, I felt the same." James nodded, then stopped abruptly. "Look, Mandy, this is where the bulldozers are kept!"

Mandy stared in surprise. The track opened out into a wide clearing, with a row of construction trailers on one side and four bright yellow earthmovers on the other. The bare earth under their feet was churned and rutted with tire tracks.

"What's the stag doing?" Mandy wondered aloud as the animal walked right into the site and headed for the biggest trailer. "There doesn't seem to be anybody here." The site seemed deserted except for two cars parked outside the trailer.

When the stag reached the trailer, he stood quietly and waited. Suddenly, Mandy heard voices. She glanced at James, who nodded to show that he had heard them, too. They crept up to the trailer and edged around the side. Above them was an open window, and now they could hear the voices clearly.

"You did a great job today. That was very smart getting there so quickly," the first voice said.

"I tell you, I went around and around that clearing until I'd trashed the whole place," said a second voice. "Nobody could find anything there, let alone a few ferns."

Mandy shuddered. The developers must have destroyed the ferns on purpose! But how on earth did they know about them? She craned her neck, but the window was too high for her to see into the trailer. She felt James nudge her, and she turned to see him getting down on all fours and pointing to his back.

Mandy nodded in understanding. Hooking her fingers over the bottom edge of the window, she stepped onto James's back and pulled herself up. Very slowly, she

peered into the trailer. She felt a huge pang of relief when she saw that both men had their backs to her.

One man had a white hard hat on — he must be one of the developer's men, thought Mandy. She clung grimly onto the sill. She wanted to see the other man. She was just beginning to lose her balance when the second man turned toward the window, revealing his profile. He held out his hand to the man in the hard hat. "Nice doing business with you," he said as they shook hands.

Mandy gasped. She could hardly believe her eyes. It was Gerald Bates!

Terrified of being seen, she dropped to the ground and rolled under the trailer. There was hardly room to move as James rolled in beside her. They held their breath when the two men came down the steps and finished their conversation. They were so close that Mandy could see the pattern on Mr. Bates's socks.

"Keep in touch," the developer said as Gerald Bates got in his car and started the engine.

"I will. See you tomorrow," the estate manager called out of the open window.

Mandy watched the car bump away down the track. She could just see the driver's face as he drove past the stag. Somehow, Mandy didn't feel surprised when Mr. Bates didn't even turn his head to look at it.

From right overhead there was an alarming thump as the developer slammed the door hard and locked it. Mandy and James cracked their heads together as they both jumped with fright. They just managed to keep quiet as the developer hurried down the steps and got into his own car. They watched him drive away, past the stag.

Only when the sound of the car had faded did Mandy and James decide it was safe to crawl out. As they brushed the dust off their clothes, the stag threw up its head, as if challenging them to do something with the information he had given them. Then, with one final gaze into Mandy's eyes, he walked off into the trees and disappeared.

"Quick, James, let's get back and tell Will what we've heard," Mandy said, starting to run down the track toward the driveway.

"You know, I don't think either of those men could see the stag." James puffed as he ran beside her.

"I'm sure they couldn't," Mandy agreed.

"Then that means —" James slowed, and he looked at Mandy, who had turned to face him.

Mandy nodded. "I think it could have been a ghost just like the fawn, James."

"This is seriously weird," James said, stopping dead in his tracks. "The stag must have wanted us to find out that Gerald Bates is up to no good."

"Exactly! James, hurry up, we must tell Will," Mandy urged, running faster as they reached the driveway. "Did you count the stag's tines?" she added.

"Yes," James said, drawing a breath. "Twenty-two!"

"Just like in the record book," Mandy said, smiling to herself.

They ran around the side of the house and across the courtyard to Will's office. But as they neared the open door, Mandy froze. Sitting casually on the edge of Will's desk, chatting to her parents and Will, was Gerald Bates!

"I agree, it's a terrible thing to lose those ferns," Mandy heard him say. "That would have saved the forest for sure. Who could have known the developers were that close?"

Mandy felt a wave of anger rising up from the bottom of her stomach. Her face felt hot. "*You* could!" she blurted out angrily as she burst into the office.

Gerald Bates stood up and glared at her through narrowed eyes.

"You told the developers about the ferns, and they went to destroy them on purpose," Mandy continued defiantly, her hands on her hips.

"Nonsense," Gerald said. "Where are you getting such rubbish?"

"We heard you talking." Mandy glanced at James, who moved forward and stood beside her.

"It's true," he said. "We heard every word."

"They don't know what they're talking about," Gerald protested gruffly. He took a step toward Mandy and James.

"Just a moment," Dr. Adam ordered, putting his hand on the angry manager's arm. "Let Mandy explain." He looked over at Will, who was sitting bolt upright in his chair. "Tell us about it, Mandy," her dad said in a serious voice.

"Well," she began, "we went up to Stagfell Pond, and on the way back we passed the clearing where the road-building machinery is kept." Mandy glanced at her mom, who nodded encouragingly. "We heard Mr. Bates and the developer talking. They said that they got rid of the ferns on purpose."

Mandy noticed that a red flush was forming at the base of Gerald Bates's neck and spreading up his face. A muscle in his cheek began to twitch. "She made it all up," he said. "Too much imagination, that's her trouble."

"We *did* hear you, and you know it's true," Mandy replied, her voice calm.

Will stood up and came around the desk to the door, his face like thunder. "Could you give Gerald and me a few minutes alone, please?" he asked.

"Certainly," Dr. Adam said. "Come on, we'll wait outside." He ushered Dr. Emily, Mandy, and James through the door, then followed them and pulled it shut.

"So it was you all the time!" They heard Will's voice clearly through the closed door. "I wondered how the developers were *always* one step ahead of me. They seemed to know my plans before I'd made up my own mind."

"You'll *never* stop that road!" Gerald Bates raised his voice above Will's. "The papers are signed and sealed. There's nothing anyone can do."

"Get out of my house and off my land immediately," Will ordered sharply. "Right now. Don't even bother to clear your desk. I'll have your things sent to you. I want you out of my sight."

"Don't you worry," Gerald Bates sneered. "I'm out of here."

Mandy heard footsteps clump across the floor, and then the door was flung open and Gerald Bates stood there, looking back into the room. "But just remember this," he threatened, jabbing a finger at Will. "I'll be back one day — the day the road is finished!" He turned and stormed past Mandy and James, glaring at them.

"Phew!" Will said as he stood in the doorway. "I didn't enjoy that." They watched Gerald Bates cross the court-yard and disappear around the house. "Unfortunately, he's right, isn't he?" Will went on in a resigned voice. "Getting rid of Gerald won't stop the road, and we haven't found any more ferns. We're no better off than we were before."

Mandy saw that Will's shoulders were sagging, and his face looked utterly defeated. "Why don't we look for another patch of ferns?" she suggested, looking from Will to her parents. "We can't be sure that was the only one. It's got to be worth a try."

"Not tonight, Mandy," Dr. Adam said firmly. "It will be dark soon." He looked at Mandy's pleading expression. "But I don't see why we can't all come back tomorrow and try again."

"Well, I suppose that would give us one more chance." Will nodded slowly. "But don't let me spoil your vacation. I've already taken enough of your time."

"We'd like to help," Dr. Adam said. "Honestly."

"At least Mr. Bates has gone," Mandy added encouragingly. "You must be glad you've found out he was cheating you."

"Yes, that's true, and it's all thanks to you two," Will agreed. He gave them a weary smile.

Mandy caught James's eye. "And the stag," she said under her breath.

Eight

Mandy's mind was racing as they drove back to the cottage. They had one last chance to save the deer park. She was determined that tomorrow they would search the woods so thoroughly that if there *were* any more ferns there, they would find them. But at the back of her mind there was a nagging worry. The developers were moving relentlessly on with building the road. And right now, there was nothing anyone could do to stop them.

Mandy pushed the thought away. She had to think positively. She thought back over the strange events of the last two days — first the fawn, then the stag, leaping out of the darkness to ask for help. Their eyes had been filled with such sadness because their home was under threat. *Please*, thought Mandy, *please let us find another way to stop the road.*

That night, Mandy couldn't get the deer out of her mind. She heard her parents come upstairs to bed, and then silence descended on the little cottage. She was worn out, but no matter which way she turned she couldn't sleep. She looked at her alarm clock. It was only two-thirty. Mandy sighed heavily and gave up trying to go to sleep.

"Mandy!" Somewhere, from a long way away, someone was calling her name.

"Mandy, wake up!" It was James, and he was knocking on the door. "Your dad says if you're not up in five minutes, we'll go without you!"

Mandy looked at her alarm clock again. Ten past eight! So she *had* fallen asleep, after all. "I'm coming!" she called out to James. She leaped out of bed, dragged on her clothes, and clattered down the stairs two at a time.

"Not like you to oversleep, dear," Dr. Adam commented, passing her a glass of orange juice. "Do you want some breakfast?"

"Thanks, Dad," Mandy said, taking a slice of toast from the plate on the table.

"OK, are we all ready?" Dr. Emily asked cheerfully, coming into the kitchen with a large canvas bag.

"Yep," Mandy said. "Today is our last chance. We've got to help Will stop that road."

"But don't forget, Mandy," Dr. Adam said gently, "you must try to keep it in perspective. There aren't necessarily going to be any more ferns. And don't forget, we'll be going home on Saturday, and after that there won't be anything more we can do."

Mandy kicked softly at the chair leg with the heel of her sneaker. She knew her dad was right.

"But I have to say, Mandy," her dad added, giving her a grin, "if there *are* any ferns growing in those woods, my money's on you two finding them!"

Will was standing outside the house, talking to two of the estate workers, when Dr. Adam pulled into the parking lot. The men wore green shirts with the words CRANBOURNE PARK printed on the front. It was still early, so there were no other visitors around. Mandy and James scrambled out of the Land Rover and went over to say hello.

"It's going to be a scorcher, I bet," Will said, looking up at the cloudless blue sky. "There's just us three and you four, so we'll need to get moving."

"That's all right," Dr. Emily said as she opened the

back of the Land Rover and took out the canvas bag. "We're all raring to go." She lifted out two bottles of water and handed them to Mandy and James. "Don't forget to keep drinking. We don't want anyone getting dehydrated."

"I think we should start our search at the ruined bridge, where Mandy and James found the first patch of ferns," Will suggested. "We could spread out in a line and work our way forward through the woods."

"Good idea," Dr. Adam replied.

Will led the way across the lawn and into the woodland, taking the quickest and least overgrown route to the clearing. It was cool and dark among the trees, and the early morning sunlight cast dappled patterns of gold on the forest floor. Mandy couldn't help feeling her spirits rise.

"OK, team, spread out," said Will as they entered the clearing. "We'll need to be about four yards apart. Otherwise, we'll never manage to cover a large enough area."

"Good luck, everyone!" Dr. Adam called as they set off slowly through the trees.

At first, Mandy could see the line of searchers on either side of her, but as the minutes ticked by and some people searched more slowly or quickly than others, the line drifted apart. She could just see James on her left, his glasses halfway down his nose and his forehead creased with a frown as he peered at the ground. He paused every now and then to lift a branch out of the way or to look under a clump of brambles.

It was backbreaking work. Even though Mandy felt she had turned over every leaf in the forest, there was no sign of the rare fern. The day was getting hotter by the hour, and she stopped to drink some water. "Please," she said to herself as she screwed the cap back on the bottle, "let us find a little one. Just a teeny-weeny one is all we need."

"Talking to yourself, Mandy Hope?" said a voice behind her.

Mandy turned to see her mom. "It must be getting to me!" she said, grinning. "Any luck?"

"I'm afraid not," Dr. Emily replied, shrugging her shoulders. "We're all going back to the house for a bite to eat. Where's James?"

"He's over there somewhere," Mandy said, twisting her head around and calling his name. "I'm not really hungry, Mom. I'd rather keep on searching."

"Hi," said James, coming up beside them, his eyes still glued to the ground. "I haven't found a thing," he confessed, looking at them and frowning. "What about you?"

Mandy shook her head. "Mom says it's lunchtime,"

she said, noting James perk up. "But I'm not hungry. You go if you want."

"No, I'll stay and keep looking," James said stoically. "It's our last chance, really, isn't it?"

"I thought you might say that, so I brought these with me." Dr. Emily handed them each a bag of chips. "It's not lunch, but it will keep you going for a little longer."

"Thanks, Mom. See you later," Mandy called as Dr. Emily picked her way back through the undergrowth. Mandy could hear loud rustling and twigs cracking on her right, which told her the others were close by. From the muffled shouts, she guessed that Will and his colleagues were stopping for lunch as well.

As the calls and rustling faded away, the woods fell eerily silent. Mandy suddenly felt glad that James was with her.

As soon as they'd finished their chips, they set off again. Soon Mandy's back was aching, her nails were full of dirt from scrabbling around on the ground, and she had a crick in her neck. She stood up straight and stretched, looking around at the endless dark greenery. There seemed to be so much forest to get through. She was beginning to think they'd given themselves an impossible task.

Mandy let out a deep sigh. Then she froze. Standing in front of her, barely a yard away, was the fawn.

She closed her eyes, half expecting the creature to disappear, but when she opened them again the fawn was still there, watching her with big, gentle eyes. "James!" Mandy called softly into the silent forest. "James, quick!"

"What is it? Have you found some?" James crashed noisily through the undergrowth toward her, then stopped abruptly when he saw the fawn.

The fawn turned, walked a few paces away, and then looked back at them.

"I think she wants us to follow her," Mandy said. "Like the stag did."

The fawn stepped daintily through the forest, her slender legs untroubled by the brambles and matted grass. She led them along a path that was so overgrown that Mandy and James had to use sticks to pin back the brambles and tangled strands of ivy before they could force their way through.

"This must be an old animal trail," James guessed as they scrambled along. At last the path began to open out and the trees thinned, letting in more sunlight. Mandy thought they were near Stagfell Pond. She stopped and looked around, trying to get her bearings.

"We're losing the fawn," James called anxiously to her as the fawn's creamy-white tail bobbed onward through the trees.

The fawn had disappeared. Mandy hurried along the trail to catch up to it. "She can't have gotten far," she said. Then she gasped. Up ahead, standing side by side in a sunlit glade fringed with glossy dark rhododendron bushes, were the fawn and the stag.

As soon as Mandy and James appeared at the edge of the clearing, the deer began pawing the ground. Puzzled, Mandy watched for a while. Then everything fell into place. "The fern, James!" she cried. "It's here. That's what they're telling us. There must be some ferns around here somewhere."

They ran into the glade and began to search franti-
cally. Mandy knelt down and brushed the leaf litter away
with her hands, working her way around the edge of the
glade. The waxy rhododendron leaves flapped against
her face and hooked on her clothes, but she kept on.
The fawn and the stag watched her silently.

Then, out of the corner of her eye, she saw a sprig of
green amid the brown leaves. Very carefully, Mandy
cleared around it with her hands and exposed three
tightly curled leaves. "James, I've found some!" she called
triumphantly from under the rhododendron bush. "Look!
This is it, isn't it?"

James hurried over. "Yes!" he exclaimed, dropping
onto his knees to help. "And look, here's some more."

Soon they had found three small patches of ferns.

"It's not very much," James said cautiously.

"No, it's not," Mandy agreed. "But, James, it's enough.
With these ferns, we might be able to stop the road!"

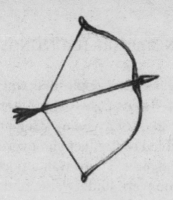

Nine

"I can't wait to see Will's face," said James. "Let's go."

"Oh, no," Mandy declared firmly. "I am *not* leaving this fern now that we've found it. You go and get the others, James. I'll stay here and guard it."

"Will you be all right?" James hesitated. "I mean, what about the road builders?"

"They won't know," Mandy said, her voice firm. "Don't tell anyone except Will or Mom and Dad."

"Right," James agreed. "I'll run as fast as I can."

When James left it seemed very quiet in the forest. Mandy sat on the ground, watching the fawn and the stag. The air seemed to ripple like water in the leaf-filtered sunlight. Then, right behind her, she heard a creaking sound, like a wire being stretched.

Mandy scrambled to her feet and peered into the forest to see what it was. There was a popping sound in her ears, as if she were underwater, and she heard the faint sound of horses' hooves thudding on the ground and dogs barking and people shouting. The sounds grew louder and louder. Mandy could hear branches snapping as they crashed through the trees toward the clearing.

Then it all became quiet. Suddenly, there was a swishing noise, followed by a dull thud. Mandy thought she recognized the sound, but at first she couldn't identify it. And then it came to her, and she flinched. It was the sound of an arrow being fired from a bow. *That must be how it was*, Mandy thought, *when King James shot the stag four hundred years ago.*

Hardly daring to look, she turned back to the deer. They were gone. Mandy had a feeling she would never see the fawn and the stag again. "Thank you," she whispered softly. "We would never have found the ferns without you."

As she stood there, Mandy began to feel the presence of other creatures in the forest. She felt as if dozens of eyes were watching her. Gradually, in the silence, she heard the gentle sound of breathing and felt the brush of warm bodies against her, as if she were surrounded by a whole herd of deer. She wasn't frightened. It seemed to her that she was being protected, watched over, by all the deer that had lived in the forest before.

In the distance, Mandy heard voices echoing. The soft bodies around her vanished. For a moment she was worried that it might be the developers, but then she heard James's voice calling her name. "Over here!" she called, waving her arms.

"We can't see you, but keep calling out, Mandy, and we'll follow your voice," she heard Will shout.

Mandy called loudly until she could see the tops of their heads. Soon, Lady burst through the bushes and rushed up to her, panting excitedly. It was all Mandy could do to keep the Dalmatian away from the precious ferns.

"Good job, Mandy and James," Dr. Adam declared as the party arrived in the clearing. "I have to admit, I had my doubts about finding any more ferns, but you stuck with it. What a fantastic result!"

As well as Will and her parents, there were several estate workers, all eager to see the ferns. The clearing seemed so crowded that Mandy was scared the delicate little plants might get crushed underfoot.

"This is the best news I've had in a long time," Will

said quietly as he squatted down beside the tiny plants. "We'll need a round-the-clock guard on these."

"We can take care of that, Will," offered a tall young man, stepping forward. "We'll work it out between us."

"Thanks, Peter," Will said gratefully, standing up. "Now I'd better get back and call Plantlife again."

"What about stopping the road?" Mandy asked. "They can't keep working now, can they?"

"We passed the trailers on our way up, and Will warned the men to stop work," Mandy's dad said. "But they told him they'll only take orders from their boss."

"Luckily, they've finished for the day, anyway," Dr. Emily added.

"We'll set them straight first thing in the morning," Will said. "Thanks, guys," he added to the three workers, who were discussing how to keep watch over the ferns. "I'll organize some food and drink and leave it in the office for you."

It was only when they started to walk back to the house that Mandy realized how tired she was.

James joined her as she trailed behind the others. "What happened to the fawn and the stag?" he asked in a low voice.

"They disappeared," Mandy told him. "I think they're happy now. They've done what they had to do."

* * *

It was late afternoon, and at the house the last visitors were making their way back to the parking lot. Tilly was waiting for them by the main entrance, and she shepherded Mandy and James straight into the restaurant, where she took bubbling hot slices of pizza from the oven. Mandy's mom and dad went with Will to the office while he phoned Plantlife.

"Eat," Tilly said to Mandy and James. "You must be hungry, missing lunch like that."

Suddenly, Mandy realized she was ravenous. "You're right, I'm starving!" she said happily, taking a bite of pizza.

"You deserve this, both of you," Tilly said with a grin as she slid more pizza onto their plates. "This is the best thing that has happened here in ages."

Mandy blushed and smiled. She knew that she and James weren't the only ones to thank for finding the ferns.

"You're a good team," Tilly went on. "You worked really hard to find that fern."

"I wouldn't have missed it for anything," Mandy said truthfully.

"Me, neither," James said with a firm nod as he helped himself to another slice of pizza.

"What do you two think about coming back again to-morrow morning?" Dr. Adam suggested when he came in from the office with Dr. Emily and Will behind him.

"The people from Plantlife will be here first thing," Will said with a broad smile. "I'm sure you'd like to meet them."

"You bet," Mandy said. "We want to see this thing through to the end."

"That's right," James agreed.

"Mission accomplished, Mandy and James," said Dr. Emily as they gathered up their things to go home.

"Yep," Mandy agreed. "I feel really tired," she confessed, trying unsuccessfully to hide a huge yawn.

"I wonder why?" Dr. Emily said, laughing. "An early night for you, Mandy, unless you want to oversleep to-morrow and miss the Plantlife officer."

"No way," Mandy said, shaking her head as they headed out the door. "I'll be here. Just try and keep me away!"

Ten

Mandy fell asleep the moment her head hit the pillow. When she woke up the next morning, she was full of energy. Linking her hands behind her head, she lay in bed for a while, her mind racing over the events of the previous day. As soon as her alarm clock showed it was seven-thirty, Mandy got up and dressed, knocked softly on James's door, then went downstairs to put the kettle on. She found a tray and put two mugs on it. James came into the kitchen as she was pouring the tea.

"You can pour some for us while I take this up to Mom and Dad," Mandy said, carefully carrying the tray up the stairs. "Room service!" she called outside her parents' room.

"Hang on," Dr. Adam answered, and opened the door in his bathrobe. "Thanks, dear," he said, taking the tray.

"What time can we go over to Cranbourne Park?" Mandy asked eagerly.

"After breakfast, if you like," her dad answered. "I know you can't wait to see what's going on!"

"You're right." Mandy grinned at him. "I can't!"

After a hasty breakfast, they piled into the Land Rover and set off along the now familiar road to Cranbourne Park. As Dr. Adam turned the Land Rover into the driveway, Mandy immediately became aware of the sound of heavy machinery grinding through the trees. "It sounds like they're still working on the road!" she said, alarmed.

"Wait and see," Dr. Emily said calmly, but Mandy noticed that her mom and dad exchanged a worried glance.

Anxiously, Mandy clutched her seat belt as they pulled into the parking lot. As soon as the Land Rover came to a stop, she jumped out and ran over to the office, with James hot on her heels.

Will was standing in the doorway, talking to Tilly. "Don't look so worried, Mandy!" Will smiled at her as she skidded to a halt in front of him. "Everything couldn't be better."

"I heard the machines," Mandy began. "And I thought —"

"It's OK," Will interrupted her. "They're getting ready to leave."

Mandy heaved a huge sigh of relief and grinned at James as her parents joined them.

"I've just had the most amazing news," Will said as they filed into the office. "My lawyer called earlier. I phoned him to tell him why I had fired Gerald, and he got a little suspicious. He rechecked all the documents and found something very interesting."

"What's that?" Dr. Emily asked.

"The signature on the authorization for the road isn't genuine," Will said dramatically, sitting down at his desk and pausing for effect.

"Is it a forgery?" asked James.

"No," Will explained. "It's actually much cleverer than that. My lawyer got in touch with a graphologist — that's a handwriting expert — and she said that nobody ever signs their name the same way twice. And the signatures on the road documents are all exactly the same, which means that somebody else must have done them, not my dad."

"Mr. Bates?" Mandy guessed, raising her eyebrows.

"Exactly," Will said with a nod. "It looks like he traced over Dad's signature and used it on all the documents. My dad might not even have known about the road. Because he used Dad's seal as well, the lawyer wasn't suspicious before now."

"That's horrible," Mandy said. She couldn't believe anyone could be so devious for the purpose of destroying a precious forest.

"There was a lot of money at stake, Mandy," Tilly pointed out. "They were paying Gerald well. Still, the police are after him now."

"And the developer, I presume?" Dr. Adam said. "He's just as guilty as Bates."

"Yes," Will said, getting up from behind the desk and peering through the window. "My lawyer is in court this morning, getting an injunction to stop the work. Look, I think that might be Ben Holmfirth, the man from Plant-life."

Mandy looked out the window and saw a gray-haired man crossing the courtyard. She followed Will and the others outside to meet him.

"And it was you who found the ferns, Will tells me," Mr. Holmfirth said, shaking hands first with Mandy and then with James. "Very good work, I must say."

"We did have some help," James began, then became

quiet when Mandy nudged him. "Well, a little — er — sort of — guidance." He trailed off lamely and shrugged, grinning.

As soon as Mr. Holmfirth saw the ferns, he recognized the species. "It'll certainly need to be protected," he told them. "It's very rare. What are your plans for this stretch of woodland?"

"Until this morning, I didn't know for sure that I could stop the road," Will admitted. "But I would like to turn it into a nature reserve, to encourage wildlife as well as let the public walk in it."

"Excellent idea," Mr. Holmfirth agreed. "We can give you any advice you need." He looked around. "This is a lovely old forest."

Mandy tapped Will on the arm. "What about the deer?" she asked. "The deer that are looking for a home. Couldn't they come here now?" she urged.

"They'd like it," James added. "A good, safe home."

"There's no reason not to," Mandy said. She knew that Will was just as eager as they were to see deer at Cranbourne Park again.

"It's Will's decision," Dr. Adam warned them. "We mustn't interfere."

"But it's a great idea," said Will, spreading his arms wide. "Just what this woodland needs."

"If they're correctly managed, a herd of deer could be very useful in a nature reserve," Ben Holmfirth agreed. "You'll need to watch out for the ferns, though."

"Let's go back to the house, and I'll phone the owner of the herd immediately. He was due to leave today, so we might just catch him," said Will.

While Dr. Emily and Dr. Adam walked back and chatted with Ben Holmfirth, Mandy and James hurried ahead with Will to make the call. In the office, Mandy listened to Will's half of the conversation. She hardly noticed her parents and Mr. Holmfirth standing in the doorway.

"That's settled then, Mr. Barton," said Will. "By the way, someone has to manage them, and we don't have a keeper anymore. Do you think Kenny would be up to the job?"

There was a pause, then Will replied, "Good. Tell him we'll see him first thing tomorrow. Thank you very much, Mr. Barton." He put down the phone and sat back in his chair. "Well," he said, smiling at them all, "it looks like I've just found myself a new herd of deer and a keeper."

Mandy punched the air with her fist. "Yes!" she cried.

"Couldn't be better," James said. "I just wish we could see the herd when they get here."

"Oh." Mandy's face fell as she realized what James

meant. "I forgot, we're supposed to be going home tomorrow morning."

"I'm sure that under the circumstances we can stay another day," Dr. Emily said, turning to look at her husband. "Can't we, Adam?"

"I think that can be arranged," Mandy's dad agreed. "After everything you two have done for these deer, you deserve to see them arrive." He grinned at Mandy and James.

"Great!" said Will. "Tell you what, why don't you all come over for breakfast tomorrow? Tilly and I will do the honors."

"That would be very nice, Will," Dr. Emily replied. "What time shall we come?"

"The herd's arriving at about seven, so you could get here to see them, then we could have breakfast," Will suggested.

"Fine," Dr. Emily said, looking at James. "If we can pry you out of your comfortable bed," she teased him, with a grin.

"Try to keep me away!" James announced. "I'll be up at the crack of dawn."

That night Mandy slept soundly and dreamed of herds of deer running through the forest. At six o'clock on the dot she woke up. She hadn't closed the curtains the night before, and the sunlight was already streaming through the window. She quickly washed and brushed her teeth, then put on a pair of shorts and a T-shirt. As soon as she was ready, she knocked loudly on the door of James's room.

James flung the door open and came out, fully dressed and ready to go. "I'm already up!" he announced.

"Great!" Mandy grinned at him. "Let's get going."

"Morning," Dr. Emily said as she and Mandy's dad came out of their room. "Are we all ready to go?"

"Yup!" said James and Mandy together, heading down the stairs and out to the Land Rover.

Mandy felt excitement bubbling inside her as they drove along the empty roads. Rays of early morning sun glinted on the chimneys of Cranbourne Park as they arrived and pulled into the parking lot. Lady came bounding over to greet them, her tail flying in the air. She trotted beside them to the restaurant, then lay down outside the door. Delicious smells wafted through the doorway. Inside, Will was behind the counter frying bacon, wearing a big white chef's hat and an apron. At the other end, Tilly was dishing out plates of scrambled eggs with sausage and toast. The estate workers were sitting at tables, eating and talking cheerfully.

"What a change in the atmosphere here," said Will as

the Hopes and James walked up to the counter. "Just a few days ago, everybody seemed very quiet. We were all really disappointed that the new road was going ahead."

"Well, you were putting on a brave front," Dr. Emily said. "We had no idea you had such worries that first day we came here."

"Seems a long time ago," Dr. Adam added, pouring himself a cup of coffee. "Still, all's well that ends well." He looked at his watch. "They'll be here soon, I think."

"We'll have to check that there haven't been any problems on the trip," Will said, then tutted to himself.

"What's wrong?" asked Mandy with a frown. She didn't want anything to spoil today.

"I didn't think of it with all the excitement," said Will, "but I probably should have arranged for a vet to be here, just in case there've been injuries on the way."

"Well, you have," Mandy told him. "Got a vet here, I mean." She grinned at Will's baffled face.

"Two, in fact," Dr. Adam said. "My wife and I will be happy to help out."

"Really?" Will said, surprised. "That would be very kind of you." He looked at them all. "You're a pretty useful family altogether. Fate must have been on my side when you decided to come here for your vacation!"

"They're here!" someone called from the door.

Mandy and James dashed outside. Coming up the

driveway was a procession of trucks, a small one at the front and three larger ones following. They stopped on the driveway near the forest edge. Mandy felt a flood of happiness rush through her as she realized that the deer were going to have a wonderful new home.

"Come and meet Kenny," Will said to the Hopes and James as a stocky middle-aged man got out of the cab of the first truck. "He was the keeper at the house that's closing down, and he's going to come and work for me now."

"Will!" the man cried, rushing forward and grabbing Will's hand. "You don't know what this means to me." He pumped Will's hand vigorously up and down. "I was dreading the thought of losing the herd. They mean so much to me."

"It's these two you really have to thank," said Will as he extricated his hand from Kenny's grip. "Mandy and James, meet Kenny Brown."

Kenny stepped forward and shook their hands warmly. "I can't thank you enough," he said seriously. "These animals owe their lives to you."

Mandy felt a lump in her throat, and she couldn't answer. She just nodded her head and smiled.

"Mandy's parents are vets," Will told Kenny. "And they're willing to help if we need it."

"Thanks a lot, but it shouldn't be necessary," Kenny said. "They were as good as gold all the way. Let's get them out, OK?" He walked toward the first truck, then turned to Mandy and James. "Want to help?"

"You bet," said Mandy. She didn't need asking twice!

Everyone watched as Mandy and James helped Kenny let down the ramp. Mandy gasped as she peered inside. There was just one huge deer inside, and it seemed to have bags all over its head.

"He's OK," Kenny explained. "Normally, I wouldn't move a deer in hard antler, but as you know, we didn't have any choice, so I wrapped bags around his antlers. That way he couldn't hurt himself — or me — when I loaded him. He's a good guy, he didn't mind."

The stag stood silently, head bowed, waiting. "I'll go in and take the bags off. Stand back when he comes out," Kenny warned as he walked up the ramp.

A few moments later, Mandy heard the clatter of hooves, and the deer appeared at the top of the ramp. Cautiously, it took a step down, feeling its way carefully. Mandy stared in admiration. It was a magnificent stag with beautiful antlers, although he was not as big as the stag that had led them to the ferns.

"He's fantastic," Will said softly from behind them. "Look at him."

"He's a royal," Kenny said. "He's big, all right, about a hundred and eighty pounds."

"A royal. That means he has twelve tines on his antlers, doesn't it?" James asked, remembering what Tilly had told them in the archives room.

"Yes it does," said Kenny.

The stag turned its head and stared straight at Mandy for a long moment. Then it shook its head and walked confidently down the ramp, past the people, and into the trees at the edge of the forest. There it turned and looked back at them.

"He's waiting for his herd," Kenny said. "Let's get them out." He waved at the other drivers, and one by one they lowered the ramps.

Mandy watched as some of the deer picked their way out nervously while others rushed out as if something were chasing them, scattering straw all over the drive. Soon the whole herd was out, snorting and skittering across the lawn on their delicate, spindly legs. The boldest of the deer started heading over to the trees, lifting their heads to sniff the clean, leaf-scented air appreciatively.

Mandy and James helped the drivers pick up the stray wisps of straw and close up the trucks.

"Come over to the restaurant for something to drink," Will called out to Kenny and the drivers as he and Mandy's mom and dad walked back to the house. Dr. Adam was already rubbing his hands together in anticipation of the breakfast that awaited them.

Mandy was helping a driver lift the ramp of the last truck when she suddenly felt a very familiar presence. *It can't be*, she thought as the driver pushed the bolt closed.

Mandy looked around. The last of the deer were vanishing among the trees, but the feeling was so strong she couldn't ignore it. "Excuse me," she said to the driver. "Could we open the truck again?"

"There's nothing in there, dear," the driver said in surprise. "I checked it myself. I counted them in and counted them out."

"Please!" Mandy persisted. Her skin was tingling with urgency.

James raised his eyebrows at her and looked puzzled.

"All right," the driver sighed. "If it will make you happy." He pulled the bolt clear and lowered one side of the ramp while Mandy held the other. "See? Nothing." The driver started to lift the ramp again.

"Hang on," said Mandy. She put the ramp on the ground and jumped up into the truck.

It was dark inside and smelled strongly of straw and animals. Mandy moved slowly forward. As her eyes adjusted to the gloom, she could make out a shape at the back of the truck, right in the corner. "I won't hurt you," she said in a gentle voice. "Come here, little one."

She heard a shuffling sound in the straw as tiny hooves

stepped toward her. Inch by inch, Mandy backed toward the ramp, coaxing the creature out of the shadows. At the top of the ramp she turned and looked down. James was standing beside the driver, waiting with a slight frown on his face.

As Mandy took a step backward onto the ramp she heard the soft tap of hooves coming closer. Slowly, the shy creature emerged into the sunlight. Mandy stepped off the bottom of the ramp and waited.

Then she heard James gasp beside her. Standing at the top of the ramp was a fawn — a fawn with a golden blaze on her forehead. She dipped her head and blinked solemnly at them.

The driver took his cap off and scratched his head. "Well, I'll be . . ." He stopped and looked over at Mandy and James. "Lucky for that little one you were here!" he remarked.

Mandy nodded silently, too full of emotion to speak.

The fawn's gentle dark eyes rested on Mandy for a moment before she tossed her head, trotted down the ramp, and disappeared into the forest.